MW01194009
LUCKY
GIRL

ISBN:978-1-7336701-6-6

Cover Design:
Giovanni Auriemma
Line Editing/Development Evaluation:
Ann Castro, AnnCastro Studio
Proofreading:
Lauren Finger
Interior Design and Typeset:
Mallory Rock

For Gar
My partner in crime

"What's one less person on the face of the earth, anyway?"
—Ted Bundy

AUTHOR'S NOTE

Portions of *Lucky Girl* are set at the historic Shakespeare Bridge in Los Angeles, California, which was erected in 1926 and deemed a Los Angeles Historic-Cultural Monument in 1974. Though the structure of the bridge is portrayed accurately in the story, some liberties have been taken with the areas surrounding and beneath the bridge to make the action more exciting. Thanks to Christopher and Erin on Facebook who graciously photographed and described the bridge for a virtual stranger!

Lucky Girl contains adult themes and is recommended for a mature audience.

PROLOGUE

A lucky girl wouldn't die like this. And she'd always been lucky. Lucky to have the kind of face that opened doors. Lucky to land that killer job. To score the ungettable guy.

Even now, she felt lucky. When she pressed her fingers to her wrist, uncertain, her pulse spoke back to her. *I'm here*, it said. *I'm here.*

A small comfort, even when the cold bit into her bones and the only sounds were her own.

Hours ago, her captor's sour breath had stung her nostrils.

"You stink."

That's when he'd taken off her blindfold, untied her wrists, and led her down a hallway to a room with a shower and a vanity mirror.

He'd watched while she ran the water scalding hot—so hot, it pinked her skin. Then he'd seated her naked in front of the mirror and pointed to a case of expensive makeup. "Make yourself beautiful."

Without protest or question, she'd complied. Already she knew better than to resist. Her defiance had left a heel-shaped bruise on her stomach that had turned a violent purple, the deep shade of an iris petal.

The lipstick she'd chosen had been used before, its red tip worn down to a flattened nub. As she'd lined her mouth, dread had turned like a worm inside her. She'd done her best to ignore it and called it hunger pangs, though he'd spoon-fed her a bowl of runny oatmeal that morning.

Then she'd stepped into the dress he'd given her, designer, satin with a slit up the thigh. His hands had lingered on her bare shoulders as he'd helped her zip it.

"Flawless."

Something she had been called before by many other men.

When he'd motioned to the small lens of a secret camera lodged high on the wall, she'd felt sick.

"I'm going to make you a star." With that, he'd shut the lights and left her alone again to wait with the steady brag of her heartbeat and the cold, slippery feel of the silk dress against her skin.

She shivered in the dark now, counting all the ways she'd been lucky.

Nothing irrevocable had been done to her. Nothing a good therapist couldn't fix. Others had survived much worse. Lucky girls like her thrived with book deals and Lifetime movies and political aspirations. They had husbands and children and lifestyle blogs. They took stunning family photographs envied by not-so-lucky girls.

The heavy lock slid open, and the door moaned. A thin blade of light sliced toward her like the point of a blade. This time when her captor stepped into the room, he wore a hood; carried a folding chair, a spotlight, and a rope.

The black handle of a knife in his back pocket mocked her.

Worse, he wasn't alone.

For the first time in her life, the world slipped out from under her, leaving her in free fall. As if the things she'd counted lucky weren't lucky at all. All her four-leaf clovers plucked. Her pennies, tarnished. Her tongue grew thick and heavy like a dead thing she couldn't swallow.

The man accompanying her captor chose to show his face. For that choice, she knew she'd suffer the consequences. As his gaze roamed her body, his lips split into a wide, sharp-toothed smile.

Her captor appeared disinterested. His eyes shone like black glassy marbles, visible in the holes of his dark hood. Nodding at the other man, he walked toward her.

"Sit."

No choice with the tip of the knife waiting at her throat. He bound her again—wrists, ankles too—and arranged the spotlight so it consumed her, leaving the other man in the shadows. Still, she could feel him there, his mouth gaping and hungry as a wolf.

"You're a lucky girl," her captor told her. "You're about to make history."

He petted her hair, smoothing it into place. Dabbed away the tears on her cheeks. Then he left her alone with the wolf-man and the camera that bore witness to it all. Its indifferent eye fixed on her.

When the time came, she didn't scream. Not because she wasn't afraid. Her whole body hummed with terror, a live wire, frayed and sparking. She didn't scream because she felt certain her audience expected it. In fact, she felt certain they would enjoy it.

CHAPTER 1

TUESDAY MORNING
8:30 A.M.
AUSTIN, TEXAS

I leave Paige tangled in the sheets, dead asleep, and five crisp hundred-dollar bills on the nightstand. That's my penance. That's how much it costs to stay sane. Because in the last twenty-four hours, I've broken three of my rules.

I tick them off one by one, like notches on a bedpost, as I knot my tie in front of the foyer mirror, and again as I slip out the door, carefully affixing the "DO NOT DISTURB" placard on the handle. I make the familiar walk of shame to the end of the hallway, to the elevators of the Obsidian Hotel, where I choose my direction. Down, of course.

To start with, I've been reckless. Even though my name—Trevor—literally means cautious. I would know. I chose it as a constant reminder. A two-syllable refrain telling me who and what I need to be. And I did try. Well, mostly tried. Nobody's perfect.

Except Paige. She's beautiful, willing, and discrete. Everything a woman should be.

Second, I've gotten too comfortable. *Comfort is the enemy of greatness*, my father used to say. Which leads me to the worst part. I broke rule number three again. The rule I've held sacrosanct since I boarded a Greyhound bus from LA to Austin seven years ago, vacating my past in a cloud of exhaust at the station: Do not become my father.

The thought of it, that I might be like him, makes me ball my fists so tight that my nails bite into the flesh of my palms. I don't even notice the man walking into the elevator until he slips in behind me. Until I've already smacked the little button—*L* for lobby—so hard the elevator's walls rattle.

"Sorry," I mutter. It doesn't feel sufficient, but the man is already frowning at me, and I don't want to make a scene. He reminds me a little of my dad with that bulbous nose and the bald spot he's still denying with a hopeful comb-over.

"Rough morning?" he asks. "Or rough night?" That sleazeball smirk. That's pure Dad, right there.

I'd like to pummel my father off the man's face, but I shrug instead. Partly because the rest of him is the anti Alan Drucker. Big and fleshy and brutish. For the rest of the ten-second ride, I pretend to care about my email, squinting at my phone's screen with the intensity of a hawk hunting field mice.

The man is still looking at me when the elevator eases to a stop at the lobby. Our eyes meet in the reflection of the stainless-steel door before it parts, opening to a drab Tuesday morning in the toothache cold of January.

I step forward first, suddenly anxious to be free of his gaze. Predatory but familiar somehow.

"Do I know you?" He speaks my worst fears aloud.

The question might as well be a gun barrel against my neck. But I don't let my body freeze the way it wants. Instead I turn to him and offer an uncertain smile.

"I don't think so." I shrug. It takes practice to seem this calm, and I wish he knew that. The level of effort it requires. "But it's a small world."

"Teddy Drucker?"

I shake my head. "Sorry, no. My name is Trevor. Trevor Dent."

He laughs—a big, hearty laugh that says he's unashamed, that shame is something for us common folk. But I don't run away. My feet stay planted like blocks of concrete. The kind they use to anchor bridges. I've prepared for a moment like this.

"Well, I'll be damned. You look just like a young man I used to know back in California. I worked with Teddy's father for a while. Always wondered what became of that kid. A real slacker. Rich off Daddy's money. You know the type."

I nod. As if this happens to me all the time. This misrecognition.

"Lived here my whole life," I say, backpedaling toward the exit. "Texas born and bred."

As if he isn't the first to see right through my expert camouflage: the blond hair I dye jet black, the brown contacts that eclipse the gray-blue of my irises, the extra pounds I'd shed like a winter coat. I'm a distance runner now. Not a slacker, no siree.

"Have a good one, mister."

As if he didn't just speak my given name. The name nobody has uttered aloud in my presence since I disappeared. Now it feels like a curse that's been loosed.

I wave at the man, flinging one arm over my head, without looking back.

My stomach careens like a runaway coaster with every intention of looping the loop, and I feel as if I'll need to duck into the first alleyway I pass and throw up last night's grilled cheese and fries, courtesy of the Obsidian's room service.

Paige abhors frills, which only solidifies her perfection. On our first *date* I'd ordered Dom Perignon and strawberries, and she'd balked. No one had ever made her feel so cheap, she'd said. Hence the classic comfort food that's *anything but* on its way back up.

But I don't loop the loop. I don't upchuck. Most of all, I don't panic. I stroll the ten blocks to my office, saunter even, reciting the three little words that temporarily keep the wolf at bay.

It's a coincidence.

It must be.

That's what any reasonable person would say. But people who disappear can't afford to be reasonable. We can't afford coincidences. Certainly not one week after Gerald Blackstone was released from San Quentin State Prison.

I'd received the Google alert last Monday—**Multimillionaire Real Estate Developer Released Following Sex Offense Conviction**—with the link to a short article in the *LA Times*. Just a few lines anybody else would've breezed right past. But for me they'd landed with the subtlety of a kamikaze missile and sent me spiraling back to the Obsidian Hotel where Paige had straddled my thighs, marked my neck with her blood-red lipstick, and left my inheritance five hundred dollars poorer than the last time.

The irony doesn't escape me. I honor it with a derisive laugh as I walk, my breath visible in the cold air. What would the late Alan Drucker say if he knew how I spent his money? *Atta boy*, probably, which only ratchets up the turning in my stomach.

It's always this way the morning after. Self-disgust clings to me like the perfume Paige dabs on her wrists, her neck. I can still smell it on my jacket. It's heaven and hell, both. But today, it's mostly hell. Last night, Paige made a confession that left me reeling—*I have feelings for you, Trevor.*

I approach the quaint one-story house in the artsy South Congress neighborhood where I've hung my shingle—DENT PSYCHOTHERAPY—for the last two years. It has a nice ring to it. Damaged and hopeful all at once. In other words, me in a nutshell.

I'll admit it's not what Theodore "Teddy" Drucker had planned for his life. The poor sucker. I'd been on the fast track to bigwigdom, eventually hoping to parlay an APD (advanced professional degree) and Daddy's connections into a fluffy executive coaching job at a global management consulting firm, where I'd use ridiculous TLAs (three-letter acronyms) like BPO and HCM and carry a Berluti briefcase and have a clichéd-but-sordid affair with my secretary (among others), just like dear old dad.

Dr. Trevor Dent has no use for those kinds of acronyms. My clients are mostly college students with FOMO, and the view from my desk is one of those photo-op street murals you see on Instagram. But I do have my own espresso machine and a sofa where twenty people park themselves each week and trust me—*me!*—with their dirty little secrets. None of which, so far, are nearly as dirty as my father's. Mine, by association.

The sound of fast-approaching footsteps stops me in the middle of the sidewalk, and I ready myself for whatever's coming. I whip around, fists balled, just as a woman jogs past me and down the quiet street lined with Priuses and live oak trees. My eyes linger on her legs, the only part of her that's bare. They're more muscular than Paige's but lovely nonetheless. Her shorts skim the curve of her buttocks and flutter around the striations of her hamstrings—her calves lengthen and contract with every stride. By the time she reaches the end of the block, my breathing has slowed, steady as a metronome. A good thing because I spot Lina waiting in her car across the street, a full fifteen minutes before our 9 a.m. session. When you're counseling an anxious client, it's advisable to be the least anxious one in the room.

I pretend not to see her. I pretend this Tuesday is off to a rollicking great start. That Lina Carr is my favorite client. As I skip up the steps with a forced grin—fake-it-till-you-make-it style—I try to quash the dread that sits on my chest. Thanks to Paige and Elevator Man, it's worse today than ever.

The key sticks a little in the lock—part of the charm of the place, the landlord had assured me—and I jiggle it a few times before it obliges and lets me inside. First stop, the espresso machine where I pop in one of the extra-strong capsules. It's going to be that kind of day. By the time I've cranked up the heat and pulled Lina's file from the locked cabinet, I'm summoned by the grating ding of the doorbell.

"Good morning, Lina." She doesn't meet my eyes as she scurries inside. "Remember, you don't have to ring the bell. You can just come in and take a seat here in the waiting room."

"I'm so sorry, Doctor Dent. I forgot. It won't happen again."

"It's alright. No need to apologize. I'll be with you in a few minutes."

Lina settles into the corner chair, her knock-off designer purse resting on her slim thighs like a lap dog. The tip of her nose is red from the cold, and I wonder how long she stood outside before she rang that damn bell.

She doesn't select any of the magazines laid out on the table nearest her. She doesn't pull a dog-eared paperback from her purse. She doesn't even scroll through her phone like most of my millennial clients, some who've been bold enough to accept a call mid-session. In fact, I've never seen her with a phone. She just sits there, waiting. The same way she has every Tuesday for the last two months.

I study her through two lenses. First, as a man. She's my type. Hell, she's anybody's type. Wavy blonde hair, flawless skin. A petite, graceful figure. Maybe it's because I'm pushing thirty, but she looks younger than her twenty-two years.

Then I consider her as a mental health professional would. She's fragile. Damaged. And I'm not that good a therapist. I should be guiding narcissistic CEOs up the corporate ladder, not reciting guided imagery scripts in an office with candles from Anthropologie. But an org psych job like that comes with publicity. The sort of exposure that would turn me and my life to dust like a vampire in the sun.

Touchy-feely it is then. At least until I put enough metaphorical highway between myself and the old me. Who knows how long that will take? It's not so bad though. My mother had always wanted to be a psychologist—to know what makes people tick, she'd say—but then she'd met my father and exchanged her dreams for his; the relationship equivalent of a colossal losing value proposition. My dad had hated the idea of his only son being a shrink, even one who worked with empty suits like him. So, really, I'd killed two birds.

I open Lina's file and scan the intake form she'd filled out herself on day one.

Name: *Lina Carr*
DOB: *1/7/98*
Age: *22*
Marital Status: *Single*
Occupation: *Student*

In your own words, why are you seeking therapy? *I need help putting the past behind me.*

Don't we all, Lina. A quick review of last week's notes reminds me why I dread our sessions more than a root canal. She's an exercise in my failures as a doctor and a man. She's the nut I can't crack.

Client presents as highly anxious and guarded. Responses to most questions are unelaborated. Reports two panic attacks this week, triggers unknown. Mindfulness tactics suggested by therapist were stated to be minimally effective. Deflects questions about history of trauma.

Then there are the things I didn't write. That she reminds me of someone from my old life. That it's hard to see past that. Sometimes I want to push her up against the wall and mash my mouth against hers until I can taste the bitter sweetness of the past. Other times I want to crush her like a rose petal beneath my heel.

When I wave her back to my office, Lina smiles without showing her teeth. She unfolds from the chair and walks toward me carefully, as if the floor is made of eggshells, not beat-up hardwood.

She sighs. "It's been a long week."

****

Lina is a vault. A safe like the one in my father's study, hidden behind a bookcase door that opened only with the touch of a secret button. Lina is just as stingy with her secrets. I've been guessing incorrect combinations, fumbling with her lock for the last forty-five minutes, but I won't be defeated. Not by this girl who looks like another girl. The one who took everything from me.

I give it one last go before our session time is over.

"I'm sensing it's difficult for you to open up. Even here, in a safe place."

"Very difficult. Especially because you're a man." She titters nervously.

"Indeed, I am. When we discussed that in our first session, I believe you mentioned it was a factor in your choosing me."

She nods, stroking the fluffy throw pillow that always ends up hugged to her chest like an armor shield. "It was a test for me. To see if I could trust you. A guy, I mean."

"And? How are you feeling about that now?"

"Well, you show up for all our appointments on time. You haven't canceled one yet."

"So . . . I've been reliable?"

"Right. And you haven't hit on me."

I'm my father's son. As much as I'd like to change that, his DNA comes hard-wired. Which means my first thought—*in my mind, I've done worse, baby*—is as crass as he was. I don't give it a voice, of course. That's where our nucleotides diverge. By the time he'd died, Dad had been through four wives, a handful of mistresses, and an honorary degree in misogyny.

"So I've respected you as a person. I've maintained appropriate boundaries in our relationship."

"Yeah, exactly. I've never thought of it that way before."

"Reliability, respect, and boundary-setting are all critical to developing trust in another person. You've been reluctant to talk about your past. But I'll assume men have let you down in these areas before. Maybe we can discuss that next week. If you're up for it."

Lina sets the pillow aside. For once, she looks me dead in the eyes. Maybe I've misjudged her.

"I won't be back next week."

"Excuse me?"

But she doesn't repeat herself. I can only watch, flummoxed, as she stands and slips a note from her pocket. It trembles in her hand like a leaf in the wind, reassuring me I haven't been wrong about everything.

"I'm starting to trust you," she whispers. "Don't let me down."

She leaves the note where she'd sat. When I pick it up, the cushion is still warm.

I unfold the sheet of notebook paper, my throat constricting as I read and read again.

I know who you are, Teddy Drucker, and I need your help. You need me too, if we're being honest. Find me tonight at 5 p.m. at Uncommon Objects. Come alone and make sure you're not followed.

When I look up, my office door is open. Lina is gone.

****

Despite legs of lead, I manage to spring up and fling open the front door. She's already positioned in the driver's seat of her little gray Toyota, strategically parked alongside a driveway entrance, so there's no maneuvering needed on her way out. Just a straight shot to freedom.

"Lina, wait!" My voice breaks the eerie quiet, sharp as a gunshot.

Though I'm certain she can hear me, she doesn't turn her head. She doesn't stop.

I'm breathing hard, ragged. Like I've done a ten-miler on the Lady Bird Lake trail, not the ten steps from my office to the entryway.

The car glides effortlessly away from me, but I can't help feeling tethered to it somehow. It's a great white shark and I'm a dilapidated fishing boat, doggedly tugged against my will to an eventual doom.

I knew this would happen someday. That I'd have to pay a price for running. Gerry Blackstone is a force of nature. A planet with a gravitational field that traps everything he wants and nothing he doesn't.

And he wants me.

I'm certain of it now.

Because as Lina makes a hairpin turn down Thistlewood, a sedan pulls out from the curb and into the street following her. It slows as it passes my office, allowing me a clear view of the driver. He looks just like Elevator Man.

****

I lock up and hoof it home, grateful my one-bedroom townhouse is a stone's throw from the office. There's no time to cancel the rest of my Tuesday clients and, anyway, I'd rather not lie to the unfortunate souls I'm supposed to be mending. I definitely can't tell them the truth.

That I wonder who will inherit their problems and the espresso machine.

That by tonight, I'll be someone else, somewhere else.

That I'm never coming back.

My house feels dark and alien to me as I move through it workmanlike. It takes less than five minutes to unscrew the downstairs air-conditioning vent and secure the go-bag I'd hidden there when I moved in. I sift through the contents of the black duffel, making sure it's all accounted for—new documents, burner cell, twenty thousand in cash, a Glock handgun, and the antique chain my father wore, the only holdover from my days as Teddy Drucker.

I suppose you might say I'm a magician, and these are my white rabbits, the tricks of my trade. This is how I'll disappear. Again.

Only this time will be different. Easier. With every iteration of myself, I become less tangible. There's comfort in being invisible but terror too. Like I'm a puff of chimney smoke. A specter passing unseen through the walls. A man with no substance, no ties.

Unless I count Paige.

She's on my mind as I toss a few T-shirts and boxers into the duffel.

Her raven hair in my fist.

As I wipe my laptop's hard drive, planning to toss the whole thing in a dumpster along the way.

Her ivory skin beneath my lips.

Even as I tug on a Yankees ball cap and check my face in the mirror, grateful for the stubble that's already shadowing my jaw. In two weeks, I'll be on my way to a full beard. And Paige will be a memory, her wide smile and the freckles she hides under too much makeup, fading like a photograph left in the sun.

With enough time, you can forget anyone. My mother died when I was seven years old. By the time I'd turned ten, I couldn't remember her laugh or that song she'd sing when she tucked me in at night. My dad forgot her too and fast. So it stings that I can't stop hearing *his* voice or seeing *his* eyes in mine.

I sling the duffel over my shoulder and hide the reminder of him behind a pair of designer shades.

There's only one thing left to do.

I find my phone on the kitchen counter and prepare it for a proper burial. A thirty-second cremation in the garbage disposal. But first I open the phone's browser and type *Blackstone trial* into the image search bar. I scroll through a few photos of Gerry Blackstone and Jordy Webber—the hotshot attorney who took my father's place—and the rest of the legal team, before I spot him.

Elevator Man.

"Fuck." I mean to yell it, but it comes out as a growl that ripples through the quiet house, reminding me just how alone I am. It's a word with sharp edges meant for my father. For Lina. For Elevator Man. For this Charlie Foxtrot of a day. For the whole universe. But mostly for Gerry Blackstone who destroyed my life. Not once but twice now.

Elevator Man had it right. We do know each other. We'd met in my other life. When I was Teddy Drucker, and he was . . . himself, of course. Because a guy like that—Erik "Gordo" Gordon, fixer extraordinaire—is unapologetically himself at all times. Even if it means getting his hands dirty by cracking a few skulls or burying a body.

The duffel slides from my shoulder and slumps to the floor. I feel as if I might be sick. As if I've been on the losing end of one of Gordo's gut punches.

Without thinking, I press 5 on the keypad. Speed dial.

"Hello. This is Spellbound Services where your fantasies are only a wish away. How can I help you?"

My throat tightens at the sound of the operator's breathy voice. I can't speak.

"Hello? Is anyone there?"

I hang up fast.

I should be long gone by now. I can't talk to Paige. I sure as hell can't see her again.

"She's a hooker, moron." I say it out loud, hoping it will help. It's the truth after all. But it only makes me feel like a scumbag. Which is the least of what I am.

When the phone rings back at me, mocking—caller unknown—I flinch. It reminds me of a bomb, that shrill little ring, a countdown to detonation. But I answer anyway. It must be Spellbound Services calling back. I'm one of their best customers.

The only reply, dead air, until a gasping, "Trevor?"

The voice is female. Frantic. Undoubtedly Paige. Though I've never heard her cry before. Like I said, the perfect woman.

"Paige? Is that you? What's wrong? Where are you?"

"You have to do what they tell you. Or they're going to kill—"

Paige wails, screams my name. Then she simply stops. As if someone pressed mute in the middle of a Liam Neeson movie. There's a shuffling sound. Like the scrabble of claws on a wood floor.

Another voice—"Hello, Teddy"—lifeless as a robot and obviously disguised. Still, it leaves me in a cold sweat, my T-shirt wet beneath my armpits. "Or should I call you Trevor now?"

"Who is this?" I croak.

"If you want to see her again, check your messages. Be a good boy and follow the instructions. Otherwise, you already know how these things end."

Even after the call disconnects, I stand there with the phone pressed to my ear. I'm a live wire, quaking, and I can't quite ground myself.

Because no matter how fast or how far I ran, the past has found me. It's here at my door, waiting to collect its debt. And I owe. Boy, do I ever.

Just as the voice promised, a text message arrives within a minute.

Deliver the Lolita files to the Shakespeare Bridge in LA at 4 a.m. on Thursday. No cops. No games. We'll be watching.

"Lolita files?" I hope that hearing the words will conjure their meaning. Will tell me where to go and what to do and how to stop Paige's scream from ringing in my ears. The only thing I know for certain: Where there's a Lolita, Gerry Blackstone is sure to follow, his fat wallet in tow. Where Gerry went, where the money went, so did my father. So did Gordo.

But Alan Drucker is long dead. And his loser son, Teddy, is nothing but a wandering ghost I can't seem to shake. Not for lack of trying.

There's no way in hell I'm going back to LA. Not for Paige. Not for anybody. I've got to save myself—and if that makes me a coward, so be it. If I leave now, I'll be crossing the border to Nuevo Laredo, Mexico by three o'clock and sipping a margarita in Playa Bagdad by nightfall.

I hope Paige will understand when I shove my cell into the waiting mouth of the garbage disposal and flick the switch. I listen to the crunch of its delicate bones and the contented whirring that follows. Then I grab my duffel and fling open the door before I can change my mind. Before the universe can fling a colossal wrench straight at my getaway plan.

"Going somewhere, Doctor Dent?"

A wrench like the lady cop on my front porch.

****

Candace Vega is just the sort of policewoman my dad warned me about. *Some broads think you're guilty just because you've got a pair.*

He'd dropped that little gem the day after he and Gerry were arrested for unlawful sexual acts with a minor. Never mind I already knew he was guilty. They both were. But to the great legal mind of Alan Drucker, guilt only applied to the things somebody else could prove.

Detective Vega perches like a peacock at the edge of my sofa, sizing me up, while her jarhead partner—whose name I can't remember—waddles around turkey-like behind her. She's already told me lies, made me promises she doesn't intend to keep.

We just have a few routine questions.

We won't delay you for long.

You're not in any trouble.

Cops have told me these lies before. In my other life. Only difference—then, I'd believed them. Then, I hadn't realized just how far Gerry Blackstone's talons could reach.

"Do you know this woman?"

Detective Vega holds her phone out to me, tapping the screen with her nail. I pretend to study the photo carefully, as if the answer didn't come as sudden and sharp as an ice pick in my spine.

I nod, swallowing hard before I answer. "Paige Penny."

She sets the phone face-up on the coffee table, with Paige's wide eyes indicting me. I look away.

"What is her relationship to you?"

"She's a friend." I'd watched my father tell that lie to my mother, then to wives two through four too many times to count. That doesn't mean I'm any good at it.

"A *friend*."

Yep, that's the look right there. The has-balls-is-guilty look. Detective Vega's got it down pat.

"A friend you pay for sex, though. Am I right?"

"Does it matter how I know her?"

Turkey grunts at me. As if he's better than me. As if he doesn't bang badge bunnies in his spare time.

"This will go a lot better for you if you're upfront with us." Detective Vega throws out another meaningless assurance. "How long have you two been acquainted?"

"Three years, give or take."

"Three years," she repeats. It sounds sad out of her mouth. Trevor Dent is nearly as pathetic as Teddy Drucker. "That's quite a long time."

I don't even try to explain. That as much as I'd been ashamed of myself, as much as I'd tried to stay away, in my warped mind

Paige is my girlfriend—minus all the hard parts, the parts I'd screw up anyway. The trust, the commitment, the expectation that I'd save her from a burning building. Rescue her from a pack of wild dogs or Gerry Blackstone's goons. Same difference.

"I guess you could say I'm a creature of habit."

"When was the last time you saw Ms. Penny?"

"We had a date yesterday evening at the Obsidian Hotel. I left her in bed this morning around eight. Is she okay?" The memory of Paige's wailing drowns out my stupid question.

"We're hoping you can help us with that."

"Me? How?"

"We believe you might have been the last person to see her. Spellbound Services contacted the hotel this morning after she didn't check in with them at the appointed time. When hotel security entered the room, they found Paige's things—her pocketbook, her makeup. They also found blood, signs of a struggle. Your name was on the reservation, and as of right now, Paige is missing."

Detective Vega lets that settle. Like radioactive dust.

"Well, I don't know where she is. She was perfectly okay—sleeping—when I left."

"And how were you? What was your mental state?"

"Fine."

"Fine. Okay." She's doing it again. Repeating what I say and making it sound borderline delusional. "We interviewed a witness—a hotel guest who was staying on the same floor as yours—who claimed otherwise. He told us you seemed upset. That you smashed around a bit in the elevator this morning like a bull in a china shop. He'd heard shouting in the room the night before."

"Bullshit." I want to tell them it's a setup. Their convenient witness, Gordo, is making sure I take the fall for this. But it sounds like something a guilty man would say. A paranoid man.

"Did you and Ms. Penny have an argument?"

"Of course not. We didn't really have that kind of dynamic." Another reason Paige was the best girlfriend I'd ever had until she went and asked for more than I could give her. "Did you say there was blood in the room?"

"So you admit it was transactional, your relationship?" *Transactional.* She's the one negotiating like a pro now. Tit for tat. Demanding an answer for an answer. Her question throws me off balance. My father used to say all relationships were transactional. Everybody wants something from somebody. Everybody has a price.

"If you want to get technical about it . . ."

"I do."

"Then, yes. I paid for her to spend time with me. You already know that. But it wasn't just about sex."

"What was it about then?" Detective Vega softens her tone and leans in toward me. She's therapizing me now, trying to convince me she's on my side.

"Companionship, I guess. I genuinely cared for her." Not that I'd ever told her. Every time I came close, I ran away.

Another grunt from Turkey, and finally he speaks, taking a kick at my duffel bag with his boot and making it clear that whatever side he's on, it's the exact opposite of mine. "You going somewhere, boss?"

"The gym. I had a break in between sessions."

"That's a mighty heavy gym bag."

As he reaches toward it, my stomach drops. As if I were teetering on the edge of a cliff with a sharp drop on either side of me. He chuckles and I lose my balance, sending rocks skittering into the abyss below.

"Do you bring your own weights?"

Snagging the handles, I muscle it out of his grasp. With it secured between my feet, I'm on solid ground again. "Something like that."

Detective Vega pretends not to notice our exchange, though I'm certain she's filed it away. "How did you typically get in touch with Ms. Penny?" she asks.

"Through Spellbound."

"So you never saw her off the clock? Never contacted her private cell phone? Emailed her?"

"No. Spellbound frowns on that sort of thing." It's the truth but not the whole truth. After our first few encounters Paige asked if I'd pay her under the table since Spellbound took twenty percent of every dollar she earned. Though I told her no, I'd started paying for her time off the clock, booking her at all hours so I could be certain no one else did. Still, our relationship is a business deal. That's the best and worst and most necessary thing about it.

"Was she in any trouble? Was she afraid of anyone?"

I shrug. I'd only seen the parts of Paige I'd wanted to. The parts I'd paid for. "She never mentioned it."

"We found traces of blood on the carpet and in the bathroom consistent with a struggle. It looked like somebody tried to clean it up. Scrubbed hard, you know. Really put some muscle into it."

"You think I did that? I walked out of that hotel this morning and went straight to my office. Did you check the security footage? I wasn't carrying a goddamn body."

Detective Vega nods, as if I've said the most sensible thing. It scares me. "You know what else we didn't see on the security footage, Doctor Dent? We didn't see Paige leave the hotel. She's not in the room you shared last night. So that's got us wondering. Where the hell is she?"

"I don't know!" My voice comes out louder and scarier than I intend. File another one away then. "I really wish I could help."

Turkey shakes his head and lowers himself onto the sofa next to Detective Vega, and I get the feeling his pea-sized brain is coming up with something. That maybe I've underestimated him.

"You ever hurt a woman?"

I picture her face. Not Paige's. But no less beautiful. I'm sure if I'd looked—which I hadn't, wouldn't—her face would still be there online. Like the last time I saw it, smack dab in the center of a MISSING poster.

"Never."

CHAPTER 2

SEVEN YEARS EARLIER
TEDDY

Teddy ducked as Nick Arrington flung the December issue of *Young Chic* at him. The magazine landed in an unceremonious heap at his feet, "LA'S MOST ELIGIBLE BACHELORS" printed across the glossy cover.

"Dude, I hate you. Like you don't already get enough action." Nick laughed, but Teddy suspected he meant it. He had reason to. Thirty thousand reasons, technically speaking. The exact sum of the financial distance between them.

Nick had been slaving away for Drucker and Webber, LLP, for five years, but the nameplate on his desk still bore the lowly title, Junior Client Relations Manager. Whereas Teddy had been hired as Senior Client Relations Manager six months ago, before the ink had dried on his college diploma. Not to mention their temporary shared-office arrangement. Teddy's dad had promised his son the corner spot overlooking downtown Beverly Hills, so as soon as Bob Fogerty retired in January, Teddy would be leaving Nick to his twelve-by-twelve jail cell.

"Whatever, man." Teddy shrugged, retrieving the magazine and tossing it on a pile at the back of his desk where he stacked all the things he didn't care about. Like the useless client surveys his father had requested. In other words, actual work.

Nick didn't need to know Teddy had bought out the whole newsstand that morning. That he'd suffered a paper cut in the eager flip to his feature on page thirty-five to confirm they'd airbrushed out the extra ten pounds his trainer, Bruce, called *love-beer-handles.* He'd made sure his dad's assistant placed a copy in the breakroom near Sidney's desk. Not on her desk, which would have been too obvious, but close enough to remind her how lucky she was to call herself his girlfriend for nearly six months now.

Nick took a bite from a doughnut, leaving a powdered-sugar mustache on his upper lip and an evidence trail of white fingerprints on everything he touched, including his receding hairline. Clueless, he pecked away at his keyboard as Teddy shook his head in disgust. No wonder he struck out with the ladies and spent most of the day side-eyeing Teddy and his full head of blond hair with utter disdain. He only had himself to blame.

"Hey, didn't you have a meeting at ten?" Nick asked. "It's fifteen after."

"Yeah, no biggie. I'm on my way."

Teddy leaned back in his chair, with no intention of getting up. Not yet anyway. Sidney had texted him. Again. Besides, he refused to be hurried by some junior flunky.

Hey! Haven't heard from you . . . Did you get my text? Are we still on for lunch?

He waited for another message, knowing she wouldn't leave it there. He'd learned early that a lot of girls have a thing for assholes. Fortunately for him, being an asshole ran in the family.

Thought we could celebrate your magazine spread at The Palm, Mr. Bachelor.

With a wicked grin—*she'd seen it!*—he clicked into his calendar to check which bullshit meeting he was late for this time. Calypso Development Group. He sucked in a pained breath, the way he did at the end of every Thursday-afternoon session when Bruce repeatedly dropped a medicine ball on his gut.

"You could've told me it was Blackstone, man." His dad's prized cash cow. Not that Blackstone would be there. He had people for that. Hell, he probably had people for his people. Still. "My dad will be pissed if he finds out."

"Like I tell my three-year-old . . . natural consequences. That's the best way to learn a lesson. Besides, you should be thanking me. I could've let you miss the meeting altogether."

Teddy met Nick's judgmental gaze head on, giving him the mental finger. He gestured to his own upper lip. "Got a little something there, buddy."

Nick looked away first, finding his reflection in the computer and wiping at his mouth with his shirt sleeve. Satisfied he'd won the point or at least evened the score, Teddy composed a reply to Sidney.

Can't. Big client meeting. But maybe I can stop by later.

Sure. The reply came so quick, he knew she'd been waiting. *We can order takeout from Fortune House.*

Teddy hopped up and gathered a handful of file folders from his stack. He had no idea if any of them had much to do with the Calypso account, but he cradled them like a shield of armor as he barreled out the doorway, giving Nick a little *up-yours* wave.

****

Teddy practiced his spiel in the elevator.

Have we at Drucker and Webber delivered exceptional value to Calypso? Are we keeping your pockets fat?

What else can we do to make Calypso successful? Who else can we screw over to fatten said pockets?

You're all welcome at the holiday party, of course. Where we'll toast to your fat pockets and ours and eat mini-quiches and make decisions we'll regret in the morning.

When the door parted, revealing the second-floor conference room, he swallowed a lump. A lone figure sat at the table, his back to Teddy. The man's navy wool suit fit his broad shoulders as if it had been made for him. Of course, it had. Probably by Tom Ford himself.

"Mr. Blackstone." His voice cracked as if he'd never quite made it through puberty. "I'm so sorry to keep you waiting. We had a crisis with the—"

"So, you're Alan's son then?"

Teddy nodded, grateful the question didn't require words to answer.

Gerald Blackstone gestured to the seat adjacent to him, and Teddy took it, keeping the files pressed close to his chest. He prayed Blackstone wouldn't ask about them.

"You were saying . . ."

Teddy gaped at Blackstone's face, impossibly tanned and unwrinkled, watching his mouth move.

"The totally legitimate reason why you've arrived twenty-one minutes late to this meeting is . . ."

"I'm sorry, sir. There's no excuse, sir."

"Teddy, do I look like an old man to you? A stuffy geezer?"

"No, of course not. You look . . ." Teddy searched for an adjective with just the right amount of kiss-ass. "Fresh-faced."

"Then, please, for the love of God, drop the *sir.* Call me Gerry."

"Will do, sir—uh, *Gerry.* I hope you and the Calypso team have been more than satisfied with the legal services we've provided. Is there anything we can do to—"

"Actually, that's why I'm here. There's a member of your staff, a paralegal, I'd like to talk to you about. I want her working closely with me on the downtown expansion project. Your father tells me she's quite . . . *talented.*"

"Of course. What's her name?"

Blackstone's lips parted in a wide grin, revealing his perfectly straight, unnaturally white teeth. Teddy knew *talented* meant young, beautiful, and eager to please. He smiled back, unable to stop himself. Until he heard the answer.

"Sidney Archer."

CHAPTER 3

TUESDAY MORNING
11 A.M.
AUSTIN, TEXAS

After Detective Vega and Turkey finish their shakedown on a painfully predictable note—"If you're thinking of taking a trip, Doctor Dent, now is not the time"—I stare at my Rolex for ten whole minutes, forcing myself to wait it out just in case they circle the block.

Every tick of those overpriced hands reminds me Paige is God-knows-where with God- knows-who having God-knows-what done to her. And that the cops think I'm involved. That I hurt her. Killed her even.

Without a body, they can't prove it. Gerry knows that better than anyone. This little show of his is all about twisting my arm. But he's capable of anything—*anything*—and if they need a body to take me down, he'll make sure one turns up.

And not just *any* body.

Paige's body.

The only body I'd known since I left LA, and I'd memorized every inch without meaning to. The burn mark on her forearm from her days working at Gino's Pizzeria. The constellation of freckles on her thigh. The scar, white and raised across the delicate blue rivers of her veins, marked by a stark semicolon tattoo. I'd googled its meaning after our first night together when I'd swore to myself that I'd never see her again.

The thought of that tattoo and what it means—that Paige is a survivor like me—makes the walls close in tighter. My lungs do the same, until my head feels light, stars spot the ceiling, and my father's ghost starts whispering in my ear.

They'll stop looking for her, Teddy.

She knew the risks.

Forget her.

He's not talking about Paige, but he might as well be. Because in a month or two, maybe less, Paige will have her own missing poster just like Sidney Archer. It'll all be my fault. I'm the common denominator.

I breathe through the sharp pain in my chest and the terrible thought that always accompanies it. I tell myself I'm not having a heart attack, and I list the evidence. Since the massive coronary that ended my father, I have an EKG every year. My calcification score is zero. I stopped eating red meat. I lost the beer gut. Christ, I'm only twenty-nine years old.

Still, there's no convincing the rabid beast pounding away behind my rib cage. It's beating so fast it's a wonder it doesn't burst.

I realize then that I can't do it. I can't run away again. I can't just leave Paige to fend for herself. One missing girl on my conscience is enough. I have to find the Lolita files—whatever the hell they are—and I'm hoping Lina can help.

In my pocket, I find her note and lay it on the table. Five o'clock is still hours away and I'm going to need every second of it.

LUCKY GIRL

****

I pilot my Mini Cooper down 71-E out of the city toward Bastrop, the little town that's destined to be swallowed by Austin someday, all in the name of progress. That's the sort of asinine thing corporate real estate guys like Gerry would say as they forced people out of the homes they'd lived in for generations. But for now, Bastrop is just the right combination of cow pastures and strip malls. A man could lose himself here. For the next few hours that's exactly what I intend to do.

I take the first exit and keep a close eye on my rearview mirror when I get right back on the freeway. I do the same at the second. Satisfied no one's following me, I make a right turn by the Dairy Queen and drive for a few blocks, cruising through the neighborhood until I select my target. A Cooper that looks similar to mine with its piano-black exterior and white racing stripes. From what I can tell, it's in decent enough condition beneath the gravel-road dust. It has decals affixed to the back window—a tiny stick-figure family—which only makes it that much more perfect.

When I'd first arrived in Austin seven years ago, I'd thought carefully about the best vehicle for Trevor Dent, perusing websites and casing car lots until I'd had the *aha* moment. It had to be a Mini, the car equivalent of a Labrador puppy. Cute, innocent, and hardly the vehicle of a man on the run. Teddy Drucker had died a little inside when I'd made the all-cash purchase. Truth be told, the old me was still holding out for a Lamborghini Gallardo. The kind of head-turner you see coming and going. The kind of car that belongs to the prick I used to be.

I pull into the space behind my mark and pocket my screwdriver, waiting for go-time. I take a few strategic breaths while my adrenaline fizzes like a shook-up soda. After my nerves settle, I pull the hood of my jacket over my head to conceal my face. Then I crack the door and emerge from my nice-guy-mobile.

The cold stiffens my fingers and fear nearly pinches my lungs shut, but I manage to swap the license plates in less than ten minutes.

Next stop, the strip mall. I toss my old laptop in a garbage dumpster and fork over $250 at Reboot Electronics for a used one. The rest of the afternoon is spent warming a barstool at PJ's BBQ, where I keep an eye on my go-bag, nurse a beer, and down a slab of pork ribs. It seems fitting that my last meal in Texas leaves a red stain on my T-shirt. A blood-colored blotch the size of a thumb. I hope it's not an omen.

CHAPTER 4

In my old life, I was one of *those* guys. Habitually late and convinced the world owed me something. And it did—a swift kick in the ass, which it had given me (and then some) in due time.

Now, I arrive early, staking out Uncommon Objects, the quirky thrift store on Fortview, from a front-row seat in my newly re-plated Mini. I need to see Lina arrive, to know exactly who I'm dealing with outside the confines of my office. To level the playing field because she'd left me reeling. But mostly, to see if Gordo is still on her tail. Or mine.

The thought of him hunkered down and watching me makes my skin crawl, even if he's no apex predator like Gerry. Gordo, like my father, is more of a pilot fish, happily scoring the great white's leftovers and doing his bidding. Whatever it takes to avoid those jagged teeth, that spine-crushing chomp. Self-preservation at its ugliest.

A steady stream of tourists and locals pass in and out of the storefront, and I study every face, searching for the familiar and dreading it all the same. Because I'm not sure what Lina expects of me. I certainly can't help her. But I need to know why Gordo was following her, what he wants with her and me and those goddamn Lolita files.

I'm no stranger to disguises. So when Lina emerges from a taxi—her head cocooned in a red scarf, her eyes hidden behind Jackie O glasses—I spot her right away. I recognize the slope of her shoulders. As if they carry the weight of the world. She charges ahead in spite of it all. I duck down, until she pushes through the front door and disappears into the store.

The taxi drives off, and I wait, sneaking glances in my rearview mirror for signs of a tail. With no Gordo in sight, I crack the door of the Mini. But I don't get out. Because Lina scares me. She's even more like Sidney than I thought—brave despite her fear—and Sidney ended up vanished, leaving me scrambling like a cockroach, hiding from the light.

I reach over and pop the glove box, sliding out the Glock and tucking it into my waistband like an honest-to-God action hero. But let's be real. The gun's been gathering dust in the A/C vent for seven years, and the only place Teddy Drucker ever fired a shot was the Elite Gun Club in LA, where he'd overpaid to pretend to be Jason Bourne while taking poor aim at a paper target. Even so, the feeling of that cold metal against my skin gives me the courage I need to go inside.

The store is made for meandering, for gawking too, and I understand why Lina chose it. Among these antiques and oddities, we'll be practically invisible. In every nook, a curiosity draws my eye. *There.*

A taxidermy fox clad in earmuffs and a fur coat.

A full suit of medieval armor.

A doll's head set alongside its decapitated body.

The foolish girl who thinks I can help her.

Lina briefly lowers her sunglasses and looks up at me with those doe eyes. "You came," she says quietly. As if she's as surprised as I am to see me here. As if she knows how close I came to blowing this town. "I wasn't sure you would."

"So you got me here. Now what?"

"Like I said, I need your help."

"With what exactly?" I direct the question to the glass figurine I've plucked from the shelf. I pretend to study it, when really I'm wondering why I came here in the first place. Paige. I came here for Paige.

"You know what, *Teddy*."

The way she says my real name, my stomach dives. When she comes closer, I swear to God she smells just like Sidney and the expensive lilac perfume I'd given her for our five-month anniversary. We never made it to month six.

"No, I don't know. And don't call me that. Ever." I return the figurine to the shelf and stalk toward the back of the store where the air doesn't smell like a lost girl. A dead girl—if I'm being honest with myself.

"Well, it's your name, isn't it? You're a Drucker." Lina hisses the name as I stare at the wall, pondering the irony of the antique ROAD CLOSED sign that hangs there.

"Not anymore. How do you know that anyway?"

"If I tell you, will you help me?"

"Help you? Why should I even trust you? You've lied to me for the last two months, and you're being followed. I saw a guy tailing you from my office when you left today."

"Erik Gordon," she says, matter-of-factly. "But you already know Gordo. Don't you, Teddy?"

I'd rather she sucker punch me. Knee me in the groin. Call me any profanity. Just not *that*. Not that name.

"Keep your voice down," I say.

"I'm guessing he's probably got his beady little eyes on you too."

"Why would he follow me?" The reasons are voluminous, of course. But they all add up to one. Gordo always finishes what he starts.

"Why does Gordo do anything?" She pauses, and I wait for the punchline. "Because his boss tells him to. His boss thinks you have something he wants. Something he *needs*."

The Gerry I know doesn't need anything. His engine runs on greed, arrogance, and the souls of dead puppies. "And what's that?"

"The files. Same as me. I just need a copy of the files."

"What files?" The word *Lolita* echoes in my head, a deranged chorus. "Even if I knew what the hell you were talking about, why would I give them to you?"

"Because I want to expose Gerry. I want to put him away. For good this time."

Gerry. Another name I'd hoped to never hear again. I turn to look at her but don't meet her eyes, fearing I've finally cracked her code. That I'll see it there. The evidence of what she's lost. But the therapist in me can't resist asking.

"Did he . . . were you . . .?"

"Thirteen when I met him. Fourteen when I started recruiting other girls to have sex with him and his friends. Better them than me, right? Fifteen when he struck that plea deal. His victims didn't even get to testify. To look him in the eye. All I want is to see him pay. I figure you probably want the same thing with what he did to you and your girlfriend."

At first, I think she means Paige. Until she removes a single printed sheet from her purse. It takes all my effort to feign confusion. To disguise the horror beneath.

Lina turns her head over her shoulder, a quick glance in both directions. She thrusts the page toward me—I don't want to look at it!—and it flutters to the floor, face-up, leaving me no choice. The familiar headline is a kick below the belt, and I wince.

Son Of Disgraced LA Attorney Named A Person Of Interest In Woman's Disappearance

Now, that it's there, exposed. I hurry to pick it up, my face growing hot as I skim the rest of the article. In my mind, I think of it as Teddy Drucker's obituary. My father's too. Because he'd died two weeks later, and I'd buried the old me in the deepest hole I could dig.

In a statement to the media, the Los Angeles County Sheriff's Department named twenty-two-year-old Theodore "Teddy" Drucker as a person of interest in the disappearance of his girlfriend, twenty-four-year-old Sidney Archer. Archer was last seen with Drucker leaving an office holiday party on December 22, 2011, at the historic Covington House, Drucker's father's Hollywood Hills' estate. Archer was employed as a paralegal at Drucker and Webber, LLP, where she met Drucker, who worked there as a Senior Client Relations Manager.

A source close to the investigation reported that Archer's parents had become increasingly concerned about her well-being since she began the relationship with Drucker, who is well-known on the LA social scene and had been voted one of LA's Most Eligible Bachelors by Young Chic *magazine. According to a source close to Archer, she'd isolated herself from her family and had been depressed. Despite an extensive search of the grounds of the estate and the surrounding hillside, Archer's body has not been found. Police suspect she was a victim of foul play. Theodore Drucker could not be reached for comment; however, his former colleague, Nicholas Arrington, recently gave an exclusive television interview describing his officemate as reckless, remorseless, and self-absorbed. "Teddy's the type who would steal your lunch from the breakroom refrigerator and then complain that you didn't hold the onions."*

Drucker's father, Alan, has also attracted police attention in recent weeks, after he and his client, Gerald Blackstone, CEO of the Calypso Development Group, were arrested on multiple counts of unlawful sexual acts with a minor and solicitation. Both men were released on bail and are currently awaiting trial.

I ball up the paper and stuff it in my pocket. I need it gone. If I had a match, I'd light it on fire.

"Ring any bells, Teddy?" says Lina.

"Don't call me that." But my eyes are already darting, certain my cursed name has reached the ears of every patron. That they're readying their pitchforks, preparing their throwing stones. They must know the awful things I've done. The things I failed to do.

"Gerald Blackstone. Alan Drucker. Sound familiar?"

I grit my teeth as her voice gets louder.

"What about Sidney Archer?"

My hand takes on a life of its own, clawing and desperate, grabbing Lina's arm and dragging her toward a dimly lit corner. She relents, cowers even. My hand retracts from her just as suddenly, shame souring in the back of my throat.

"I'm sorry. It's just that I didn't . . . I'm nothing like my father. Nothing like Blackstone. I didn't kill her. The cops never pressed charges. They had no evidence. They didn't even find her body." I've never sounded so guilty.

But Lina nods at me, biting her lower lip to stop it from quivering. "I know," she says. "They never will. Not unless Gerry wants them to."

I stare at her, questions multiplying in my brain like a virus. When I try to find her eyes, her answers, behind those dark lenses, I spot my panicked face in the reflection. Behind it, a semitruck of a man in a black suit, barreling toward us.

I spin around as Lina curses under her breath. There's nowhere to go. We've boxed ourselves in.

The man must sense our fear, because he slows his roll and holds up his hands, as if to say he means no harm. In one of them, he flashes an official-looking ID, too fast for me to read his name.

"Doctor Dent, I'm with the FBI. We have reason to believe you're in grave danger. You need to come with us immediately. You too, Ms. Carr."

Us.

Another man, in an identical suit, materializes behind him. They're both wearing earpieces to go with their matching side holsters and shiny bald heads. Both have a small gold trident pinned to a lapel.

As the store patrons gasp and gawk and whisper, the men flank Lina and me and maneuver us down the narrow aisle toward the front door, where the setting sun streams in, momentarily blinding me. I shield my eyes and turn to Lina. But she's staring ahead, her whole body clenched tight, like a frightened animal that might bolt at any moment. I wonder if she's thinking what I'm thinking.

How did they know our names?

How did they find us?

What now?

The door is opened for me, and I step through it.

"There," Baldie #1 tells me, pointing to the gravel alleyway alongside the store where I spot the black SUV that's meant to swallow us. It has tinted windows and its sleek, dark body is the color of a vampire's cloak.

"Uh—" I pull up short of the vehicle, wresting my arm away from him. "Can we discuss this for a minute?"

"There's no time, Doc. We can talk in the car."

Baldie #1 grips my forearm, more forcefully this time, jostling me in the direction of the SUV. With his free hand, he opens the door, and I gaze into the gauzy blackness. It's a cave. A mouth waiting.

I consider reaching for the Glock, but I don't stand a chance in a shoot-out. And hand-to-hand combat is out of the question, because this Baldie's jaw is so chiseled, I'd swear he eats shrapnel for breakfast.

War of the words it is, then. Lucky for me, I'd earned a 750 on my SAT Verbal, after my dad coughed up a couple grand for a private tutor with Lois Lane sex appeal. Six months later, she became his wife number three. One year after that she'd added an *ex* to her title, just like the two who came before her, including my mother.

"Listen, I'm not getting in until you tell me what the hell is going on here. I don't even know your name." I shake off his arm and back up, looking for a place to run. Looking for Lina.

Baldie #1 nods, surprising me. "You're right. I'll explain everything."

I should feel relieved, but he has the eyes of a shark. Cold and dull and soulless. As he closes the distance between us in two strides, my stomach takes a nosedive. I start to bolt, but I slip on the loose gravel. Fumble for my gun, but it's too late. He's got the jump on me, and the barrel of his weapon prods my rib cage.

"Drop it. Now."

I set the Glock on the dirt, glancing beneath the car to the other side, where I find Lina's sneakered feet spread-eagled, and Baldie #2's boots firmly planted behind her. I can't see his hands, but I'm certain they're taking liberties. Exploring her body, caressing her hips, running the length of her legs. All under the guise of searching for a weapon. I hear Lina curse at him, and I feel sick. But my Glock has already disappeared into Baldie #1's waistband.

Unsteady with dread, I shuffle forward. One step at a time. Toward the SUV that may as well be a hearse.

"Get in." He doesn't wait for me to comply. He shoves me forward, and I brace myself, staring at my hands against the smooth black leather. Expensive but practical. Easy to clean. Blood will wipe right off. It turns out you can clean up anything but your filthy conscience.

As I lift one foot from the ground and place it on the floorboard, stalling, a hard thwack snaps me to attention. A bald head skids down the pane opposite me, the cheek smooshed, the mouth silent but contorted in pain.

Beside him, Lina, with a small device in her hand jammed into his thick neck. I try to make sense of her—*this* Lina—not the timid girl from my therapy couch. As Baldie #2 slumps to the ground, she ducks down, out of my sight.

Still, her voice carries. "That's what you get, asshole. Next time, keep your hands to yourself."

A part of me hopes she'll come around the corner, armed with her stun gun to make quick work of Baldie #1. But my father lectures me in my head. *I didn't raise a sissy. You don't need a woman to rescue you.*

I spin around, fists clenched. Now I'm ready for a fight. Too bad it's not Alan Drucker but Baldie #1 in front of me. Too bad he's still got a gun. Two, actually. I hurl myself at him anyway, landing like a BB against the cement wall of his abdominals.

"Guess you're not with the FBI, then," I say, listening to the faraway rumble of ironic laughter that must be mine. It's the last sound I hear.

****

Turns out heaven looks a lot like Austin. With a wide blue sky and a legion of pickup trucks and the distant sound of honky-tonk music playing. An angel greets me where I lay. Her halo, a cascade of blonde hair that falls toward my face. When she gazes down at me, the throbbing pain in my temple stops completely.

Instead of a prayer, I offer up a name. A name I haven't dared speak aloud since I left LA. This angel must be her. It's a miracle because she's not even mad at me.

"Sidney."

"Get up. We gotta go."

She lowers her hand to my face, and I wait for the gentle caress of her fingertips. For her to tell me it's okay that I didn't believe her. Didn't protect her. Hell, I'd walked her straight into the lion's den.

"Trevor. Snap out of it."

Three stinging slaps to my cheek. That's what it takes for me to realize I haven't died.

I'm not in heaven.

This girl is no angel. She's certainly no Sidney.

The parking lot spins as I bolt upright and grab Lina's wrist before she delivers another smack.

"Alright, alright. I'm with you."

I understand then why she's panicked. Why she's urging me to get up, her eyes wide with desperation.

The Baldies are gone. So is the SUV. I'd think I dreamed the whole twisted episode if not for the spot of blood on my fingers when I touch it to my forehead.

A small crowd has gathered around, a few dead-eyed onlookers training their phones on me. Like I'm just another oddity, another uncommon object. A siren screams in the distance, growing louder, until its insistent wailing judders my bones, and I spring to my feet. I motion to Lina, and she follows me back to my car. Breathless, I fling myself inside and fire up the engine just as the first police car arrives at the storefront.

The officer emerges with the practiced calm of someone who's used to this sort of thing. To flashing red and blue lights and thwarted kidnappings and crowds with cell phones. To wide-eyed people pointing at the empty alleyway and past it.

At me. At us.

I turn to Lina, notice the gun in her hand. She must've lifted it from Baldie #2 before we ran. She tosses it beneath the seat, and

I stare at the floorboard, stuck on trying to figure out how I got here and why.

"Go!" Lina yells, pounding the dash.

I throw the Mini in reverse and peel down the street, taking the first left turn so fast, I nearly run into the ditch. A quick right and I veer onto Ben White Boulevard, white-knuckling the steering wheel. My pulse is a hot rod, burning rubber down the track. But the rest of me is stuck in five o' clock traffic. I lay on the horn in frustration.

"Is that cop behind us?"

Lina cranes over the head rest. Her first answer, an exasperated sigh. "What do you think, genius? You tore out of there like you stole it."

"What was I supposed to do? Besides, you told me to go." I sneak a nervous glance into the rearview mirror to confirm, wincing when I see the purpling bruise on my forehead. Sure enough, at least one of the fine officers of the Austin Police Department is on our tail. Where one goes, the others will follow. Thank God for stolen plates.

I rev the engine, but there's no escape, so I maneuver to the shoulder, rumbling over the rough terrain. Gravel and glass and God knows what else spits out behind us. I grit my teeth because it's too late to swerve, and the car flattens a wayward traffic cone.

"I thought you'd be better at this," Lina mutters.

"At what exactly?"

"Staying alive. Fighting off bad guys. Driving."

"Thanks for the feedback. I'll be sure to add those to my self-improvement checklist. What happened back there anyway?"

"A mini stun gun is a girl's best friend." She holds up her foot, pats her sock. "After I dropped that guy and you got yourself pistol-whipped, they turned tail. His partner lugged him into the back seat, and they got the hell out of there. The crowd probably spooked them. Hooray for cell phones and busybodies, right?"

"Hooray," I echo weakly, my voice as thin as a thread. Because those same busybodies are no doubt plastering their images of us on their Facebook pages right now.

As we rumble past the next turnoff, Lina grabs the wheel and steers it to the right. I let out a childish yelp when the Mini veers down Russell Drive.

"What the hell?"

"We have to get off this road. I know where we can lose him. If you can make this thing move, that is."

Lina snorts as I press the SPORT MODE button near the console, giving the motor a much-needed kick, and the car jolts forward. She directs me right, then left. Then right and left again. I don't dare look in the mirror. Don't take my eyes from the road. I barely breathe.

"In here," she says, pointing me into a grocery store parking lot. "Find a spot. Quick."

I zip into the first open stall and cut the engine. Following Lina's lead, I duck down low in the seat, peering up into the side mirror. I've watched enough cop shows to know exactly how this will go down. Me, hands stuck out the window, fumbling for the door handle. Flinching as some cowboy officer barks his orders at me. Me, on my knees on the pavement, my wrists cinched behind my back. I'll be carted away to the clink where Detective Vega and her wattle-necked partner will lock me in a windowless room and hurl their questions at me until I confess.

"Are you alright?" Lina asks, nudging me in the ribs.

I should be the one asking that question. I'm the therapist here. She's the one with the DSM diagnosis; unspecified anxiety disorder with panic attacks.

"Of course I'm alright." Even I can hear the hitch in my voice as I say it. "The cop . . .?"

"He drove right past. I told you he would."

Relieved, I sit up, trying to coax my heartbeat back into submission with the same mindfulness techniques I dole out to my frazzled clients. I wonder if Zen has its limits though. When your whole life is upended, what good is being in the moment? Still, I listen to my breathing and focus on a gray-haired woman trailing behind a red shopping cart. She steers it clumsily toward the station wagon in front of us, where it bumps against the side panel and comes to a rest.

"What now?" I ask, watching the old lady struggle to lift a case of diet ginger ale. Her arms shake like twigs under the weight of it.

When Lina doesn't answer, I turn to look at her beside me. Her eyes are fixed on her hands in her lap where she's fidgeting with the ID badge she must've lifted from Baldie #2. He stares back at me, his name and details typed below a photo of his stoic face, set atop a hologrammed image of a trident: DEREK CRAIG. SENIOR SPECIAL AGENT, POSEIDON SECURITY.

"Did you know that guy?"

Lina's bottom lip quivers as she shakes her head. I should feel bad for her, but her little meltdown is reassurance. Proof she doesn't have ice in her veins, and I'm not as hopeless as I thought.

Across from us, the old woman shuffles back to her cart. She loops the handle of the first grocery bag around her wrist. It swings back and forth like a pendulum as she walks. Finally, when the woman reaches her car and drops the bag onto the seat, Lina answers.

"But I do know Poseidon. They're a private security firm."

"A private security firm? What would they want with us?"

"Wow. You really are clueless." Just like that, she's back. Smart-ass Lina. The side of herself she'd kept as cleverly disguised as a scar. "A lot of powerful people want your dad's files. They're legendary. Surely, you must know that."

I count the things I know about my father. It's a short, sad list.

Lawyer. Adulterer. Pervert. Snake.

"We weren't close."

"But you'll help me get the files, right? You know where they are?"

There's something wild in Lina's eyes, a flash of desperation. A lightning strike of panic. This is my client. This is the girl I recognize.

"I have a hunch." Which is total bullshit. Until today, I'd never heard of the Lolita files. But there are answers I want from her too. Answers I'd given up on until about an hour ago. "But I can't make any promises. Not until you tell me everything you know about Sidney."

Her jaw tightens. "I will. I swear. Not here though. Not now. We should—"

In the rearview mirror, I spot the reason for Lina's sudden silence, and my own throat constricts.

The thugs from the store are back. Their black SUV idles behind us, blocking us in. Derek Craig stalks toward the passenger window, his partner right behind him, guns drawn. When he reaches the door, I spot the stun-gun marks on his neck, two perfect circles. Two fang bites, raised and red. He looks angry as hell about it.

"Let's try this again, shall we?" As if we have any choice in the matter.

He jerks the handle, and Lina cries out, ducking down as she reaches beneath the seat.

"We need the files, Lina."

He raises *my* gun, aims it at the glass. Lina points hers back at him. The old woman screams, bumping the cart in her attempt to get away. It careens down the lane and through the parking lot toward freedom. I wish I could do the same.

I jerk the car into reverse and step on the gas, propelling it backward. The impact is harder than I expect. It jolts both of us forward. Me against the steering wheel, Lina into the dash. I lose my breath, and the gun tumbles out of Lina's hand and onto the floorboard.

Derek rapid fires, the first bullet pinging off the side panel. The next two off the hood. But his partner waits, steadies himself, and aims the barrel at Lina. She scrambles for the gun, but it's too late. I know it.

I close my eyes and wait for impact. The shattering glass. The blood spatter. I'll be next. Teddy turned Trevor meets his end in a grocery store parking lot. For what? Files I've never seen. Files that belong to a dead man I don't want to claim as mine.

A single shot cracks the stillness like a fissure in the ice.

Lina must be dead. But I can still hear her ragged breathing.

When I will myself to look, she's right there next to me. Intact. Tears and mascara running down her cheeks. The gun, unfired, at her feet where it fell.

In the rearview, Derek cowers, blindly returning fire as he runs. He rushes to the SUV and speeds away, leaving rubber marks and an uneasy silence.

"Where's the other guy?" I ask.

"Back up," Lina says.

Which isn't an answer, but I do it anyway. I feel hollow inside, a husk blown about by the wind. There, on the pavement, is Derek's partner, slumped against the parking block with a bullet hole in his head. I follow Lina's eyes to that runaway shopping cart and past it, to the dark sedan gliding away. Gordo at the helm.

"Drive," Lina tells me.

****

Lina makes me nervous. It's as if she already knows where we're going. I could still show her up. Turn tail, head south to Nuevo Laredo. Then I'd be no better than my father, looking out for *numero uno.*

There are only two cities in the world Alan Drucker felt at home. Two places he'd bury the carcasses of his secrets. And both of them are west of the Rockies. It makes sense that these legendary Lolita files must be there too.

I guide the Mini onto I-10 West, careful not to exceed the speed limit. Dread pricks at the back of my neck, and my eyes keep drifting to the rearview.

When Lina spots my go-bag in the back seat, she makes a reach for it. But I grip her wrist hard, and the gun falls back to the floorboard.

"I was only going to put it in the bag," she says. "For safekeeping."

I don't let go, one-handing the steering wheel like a man possessed. Disgusting as it is, I'm still a Drucker at my core. I know how to control a woman. I turn the tables on her.

"That guy, Derek. It seemed like he knew you. What aren't you telling me, Lina?"

She wrestles her wrist free and glares at me. "I could ask you the same. I'm sure you have plenty of secrets."

I think of what I've done. First, to Sidney. Now, to Paige. If Lina knew that, she'd hand me over to Gordo herself and watch him pull me apart limb by limb. "Fine. Think what you want."

Lina shrugs, and I stare straight ahead, wishing I could change things. Not knowing where I'd start.

"Las Vegas, first," I tell her, answering the question she still hasn't asked. "Sin City."

CHAPTER 5

SEVEN YEARS EARLIER
SIDNEY

Sidney's cell phone beeped from the nightstand, waking her like a shot of cold water. Removing her sleep mask, she rolled over and reached for it, knocking a stack of legal contracts to the floor. That's what happens when you take your work to bed. You wind up on your knees in the dark sorting through one hundred pages of Drucker and Webber's legalese.

Still, she had to check the phone. With her empty-nester parents pushing sixty and no siblings to rely on for back-up, the worrying fell squarely on her shoulders. And worry she did. The worst news always arrived after midnight. And it was at least a three-hour drive from her place in Venice Beach to her childhood home in Kernville.

You up?

She groaned, half annoyed, half excited. Teddy Drucker had a way of doing that to her.

Now I am.

In an instant, he replied. *I'm downstairs with takeout. Buzz me in.*

I have an early morning. Really early. And you're late.

But already, she'd swung her feet off the bed, combing her fingers through her honey-blonde hair in the full-length mirror.

C'mon, you know you want to be bad. Plus, I have news. And those edamame dumplings you like.

After spitting a swig of mouthwash into the sink, Sidney pressed the entry button. She knew she'd pay dearly come morning. But LA's most eligible bachelor had landed on *her* stoop, even if he had promised to arrive hours ago. Sleep could wait.

"Hey, beautiful." Teddy leaned in the doorframe, still in his suit. His tie hung undone around his collar, and he smelled like beer and cigarettes. But those slate-blue eyes drew her in.

"Yeah, yeah, yeah. Don't try to sweet-talk me when you're drunk."

Teddy stepped across the threshold and into her apartment. A studio the size of his living room, though he never seemed eager to be at Covington House, the sprawling mansion he and his father called home. The few times he'd taken her there, she understood his avoidance. It had the shimmering face of a diamond but a cubic-zirconia soul.

He laid two bags from Fortune House on the coffee table that doubled as the dining room. "A couple of my Kappa Sig buddies are in town. They insisted on buying me a round after the Lakers game. Did I tell you my dad has courtside seats?"

He had told her, of course. Several times. Sidney didn't mind his bragging. She found his insecurities endearing, irresistible even, especially when he flashed that boyish smile. Even though she still couldn't fathom why he felt the need to impress *her*, a small-town girl without a trust fund.

"Right by Jack Nicholson's, you said." Sidney joined Teddy on her futon, a holdover from her college dorm, and pawed through the bags searching for her favorite item. "Did they win?"

"It was a blowout. Kobe really put on a show. Thirty-one points and seven assists." Teddy reached into his jacket pocket, holding two individually wrapped fortune cookies in his palm. "Looking for these?"

She grabbed for his hand, but he held it just out of her reach, teasing her. Not that she minded.

"You've got to pay the toll first." He leaned in closer, kissing her lips, then deposited the cookie in her lap.

Eager, Sidney pulled open the plastic wrapper.

"Wait," Teddy said. "It's bad luck to eat them first."

"Since when are you so superstitious?" But she acquiesced, surrendering the small package to the coffee table as Teddy set it with their greasy cartons and plastic silverware. "What's this big news you wanted to tell me?"

"Remember that client meeting I texted you about? Well, it was with Gerald Blackstone." Teddy spooned the plumpest dumplings onto a paper plate and slid it in front of her.

"*The* Gerald Blackstone? As in, your dad's best client?" Whenever Sidney heard that name spoken in the office, it resonated with quiet reverence. Or blatant panic. Upsetting Blackstone seemed the surest way to earn a pink slip.

"As in, *your* new client. You've been assigned to help with the Calypso downtown expansion project at his request."

Sidney stopped mid-bite. "What?"

"I already talked to my father, and he okayed it. Blackstone asked for you specifically, Sid. He said you're—and I quote—quite talented. You're big time now."

Sidney laughed, her excitement bubbling over. Finally, someone saw her as more than just a pretty face. Someone noticed her skill. Her diligence. Her damn hard work. A recommendation from Gerald Blackstone would open the doors of any law school in the country, including her reach school, USC.

Before taking another bite, she tempted fate, ripping open the plastic wrapper of the fortune cookie and breaking it in half. Teddy shook his head at her, sporting a rueful grin, as she unfurled the tiny paper with her fortune.

"Weird." Her voice sounded strange, flat. "It's blank."

Teddy said nothing.

"What do you think it means?" she asked.

He made a ghoulish face at her, humming the sound of impending doom. “Oh, c’mon. It doesn’t mean anything except that the printer failed. The ink went bad. Human error.”

But Sidney had already grabbed for her phone, typing her question into the all-knowing Google. After a moment of searching, she looked up at Teddy, her heart sinking a bit.

“My future is undecided.”

CHAPTER 6

TUESDAY EVENING
9:30 P.M.
SONORA, TEXAS

Interstate-10 West unfurls like a dark ribbon toward the horizon, taking Lina and me through the heart of rural Texas. Nothing but dry pasture on either side of us for hours now, a canvas of black sky above.

A few drops of cold rain spatter against the windshield, and the radio fritzes in and out until finally it's nothing but static. Lina still hasn't mentioned Sidney or given up the answers she promised. But to be fair—chicken shit that I am—I haven't asked. And after the way I acted, grabbing her arm like that again, I can't blame her.

I finally break the long silence, pointing to the road sign up ahead.

SONORA 8
EL PASO 380

"Only six hours till El Paso."

"Only? Does this state ever end?"

I'm relieved to hear a spark of life back in Lina's voice. But her question gets me thinking, worrying. It'll be at least another sixteen hours before we reach Las Vegas, and I have no clue what to do once we get there.

For the first time in years, I wish my dad hadn't kicked the bucket. But I quickly reconsider when I remember what he's done to me. What he's still doing. Here I am again, paying for his mistakes. Paige is paying too, just like Sidney.

I smack the steering wheel, and Lina takes in a sharp breath, her hands coiled tight as springs in her lap.

"Guess it wasn't all an act then? Your anxiety?"

She levels me with a look. Her eyes shine in my periphery, hot as stones, before she speaks. "We need to stop soon. Get a new car. Some new clothes. They'll be looking for us."

"The cops, you mean?"

Lina laughs at me. "The cops are the least of our problems. They have rules to follow. Poseidon makes their own. As do whoever hired them. Let's just say, rules are for us common folk."

I remember a time when I was anything but. When I floated above it all, looking down my nose at anyone who made less than six figures.

"Do you have any idea who hired Poseidon?"

"Somebody with a helluva lot to lose. Blackstone kept records on all the girls, the men who paid to be with them, and the kinky things they liked. He made bank on it too, extorting those rich pervs for his silence. The Lolita files are Blackstone's leverage—always have been—and now that he's out of prison, he's ready to use it."

"So that's why Gordo came to our rescue. He needs us alive to find the files."

The whole sordid plan took shape in my mind. A ledger of the dark deeds of the wealthy and powerful. My father must've salivated knowing Blackstone had entrusted it all to him.

Lina gestures up ahead to the first city lights we've seen in miles. Another passing sign welcomes us to Sonora, Texas. Population 2,672.

"Pull off here. In a small town like this, everyone leaves their cars unlocked. It'll be easy to boost one," she says.

I nod, as if I do this all the time. But as I take the next exit, I'm hoping Lina doesn't expect me to do the boosting. Stealing a license plate had already pushed my criminal sophistication to its limit. I double back toward the strip mall, then make a loop on the feeder road, checking the rearview for indications of a tail.

"We're in the clear," Lina assures me. "For now."

"How can you be so sure?"

Lina rolls her eyes, shakes her head. "Because we're still alive, Doctor Dent. That's how. Poseidon doesn't mess around. Especially not after what happened back there."

At least she's not calling me by my old name anymore. But the way she enunciates those three syllables, I can't say I like this one much better. She directs me into the nearly empty Family Dollar parking lot. A single light pole illuminates the few spots nearest the door, leaving the rest in inky darkness.

I position the Mini close to the exit. "Is this really the best place to steal a car?"

Wrapping her scarf around her head, she cracks the door, letting in the cold, wet air. "We're not getting a car here. C'mon."

Reluctantly, I tug on my Yankees cap to cover the bruise on my forehead. Then I hide the gun in the go-bag as Lina intended, grabbing a wad of cash from inside it, and follow her through the spitting rain toward the gleaming windows of the store. Their fluorescent brightness scares me. There's no hiding here.

I join Lina beneath the awning where she's taken refuge. "You should know better than anyone how to disappear. If we want to make it to Vegas, we'll need to change our appearance. Those videos of us from Uncommon Objects are bound to be all over the internet by now."

She's right, of course. I do know how to disappear. Though apparently not well enough.

Inside the Family Dollar, we make our way past the last-chance sales racks of leftover holiday décor toward the clothing aisle while a nineties pop song plays over the speakers. Lina moves like a pro. Sizing me up, she shoves a Texas Longhorn sweatshirt and a black stocking cap against my chest. For herself, she selects a denim jacket and a powder-pink baseball cap. She completes her girl-next-door look with a pair of tortoiseshell reading glasses.

"I'll meet you in the front," she says, heading for the beauty aisle.

At the store's entrance, the door opens, and a man strides in, bringing a fresh blast of cold air with him. I find myself gaping at the holster on his narrow hips. At the gun resting inside it. He dries his boots on the mat and waves at the middle-aged cashier before he picks up a basket and saunters toward the refrigerated section. He looks harmless enough, studying a carton of milk beneath the brim of his cowboy hat. It's what I can't see that unnerves me.

My eyes dart, as I scuttle toward the register and force a smile at the woman behind the counter. Her well-worn nametag proclaims her Glenda, Assistant Manager.

"It sure is getting bad out there." She gestures over her shoulder to a portable television, WINTER STORM WARNING scrolling in red at the bottom of the screen. "Hope you don't have far to go."

My answer gets stuck in my throat. I'm not as smooth as I thought. Watching a man take a bullet to the head will do that to you.

"Not far at all. Right, honey?" Lina appears beside me, her arm snaking around my waist.

But it's Paige's I imagine there. She's the only woman who's touched me like that, with familiarity, in years.

"We live just down the road," I blurt out, without thinking.

"Funny." But Glenda isn't laughing. She's studying us now with thinly veiled suspicion. The clothing, the scissors, the hair dye Lina's laid on the counter. "I haven't seen you two here before. You new in town?"

"He means the next town over. Roosevelt. We're just passing through."

I'm glad Lina paid attention. We'd eclipsed Roosevelt in all of ten seconds, just a blip on the highway. But I don't feel relieved.

I watch in horror as a news anchor appears on the screen behind Glenda. Thankfully, she's got the thing on mute. Because there we are in all our glory. Me, getting pistol-whipped like a milksop while Lina drops Baldie #2.

There's a new warning scrolling now: PERSONS OF INTEREST SOUGHT IN CONNECTION WITH GROCERY STORE HOMICIDE OF PRIVATE SECURITY FIRM EMPLOYEE JOE KIEFER.

"Can I get anything else for ya, hon?" Glenda nearly turns around to see what has me so transfixed.

But, lucky for me, Lina *is* smooth. "A pack of Camels, please."

While Glenda busies herself at the register, Lina crushes my foot with the toe of her boot. She gives me a pointed look when I grimace.

"That'll be seventy-one dollars and twenty-three cents." Glenda looks at me expectantly.

I pull the stack of bills from my pocket, fumbling to count out four twenties, and watch helplessly as a few flutter to the ground. Approaching footsteps sound like a death knell, and I realize I'm about to blow it again.

"Finders keepers." The armed cowboy grins at me, claps me on the shoulder hard enough to rattle my teeth. "Just kidding."

"Sheriff Bennett," Glenda scolds. "Don't you give these lovebirds a hard time."

Chuckling, he lays the bills on the counter with a nod, but I can feel his eyes on my shaking hands while Glenda retrieves my change. Lina stays calm, chatting with them both about the weather and helping Glenda bag our disguises. Meanwhile, I'm certain beads of sweat have broken out on my forehead.

I walk as fast as I can on wobbly legs, letting the sleet pelt my flushed face. It's coated the asphalt in a shimmery white that crunches beneath my shoes.

"What the hell was that?" Lina hisses once we reach the Mini and close ourselves inside. She rubs her hands together for warmth. "I *really* thought you'd be better at this."

"Yeah. You mentioned that."

"Well, I don't get it. You've been Trevor Dent for years now. Why so squirrely?"

I rev the engine, wanting to get the hell out of here and back on the road. To put as much highway between me and Austin as I can. "It's been a bit of a rough day, in case you haven't noticed. The cops probably think we killed that guy."

"That's why you're losing your shit?"

"That's one of the reasons." Paige's scream drills through my brain like a hot nail. I can't stop it. Detective Vega and her turkey-necked partner are sure to have seen that video too. They'll know I'm on the run. They'll make assumptions. "Your little stunt at my office didn't help. We could've talked there, you know. Avoided this whole mess."

"I needed proof I could trust you. Proof that you cared." Lina looks past me, her eyes suddenly wide. I turn toward the window as the sheriff pounds his fist against it, echoing the hollow thud of my heart.

Be cool. I can do this. I captained the Dunbar Academy varsity lacrosse team to two state championships. I talked Dean Willits out of suspending Kappa Sig when two of our pledges ran naked through the quad. For Christ's sake, I bailed my perverted father out of jail without batting an eye. I need to get my shit together.

I press the button, and the window slides down, sticking slightly in the icy rain. "Is everything okay?" Somehow, I manage to sound the exact opposite of panic-stricken.

He leans in, the smell of his tobacco breath wafting in on the wintry wind. "I reckon it's hard to get much traction with those small tires. Be sure to keep it under the speed limit and watch out for black ice."

"Of course, Sheriff. We'll take it slow."

"Y'all get home safe." He taps the roof once before he crosses the lot to his pickup truck.

I let him drive away before I guide the Mini back onto the feeder road. Once we leave the Family Dollar in the rearview, Lina throws her head back and laughs.

"Finally, you pull it together. And just in time." She mimics my casual *Of course, Sheriff.* "I was beginning to think you weren't a Drucker after all."

That settles about as well as a boulder in my stomach. Because I can hear the bitterness in her voice. It makes me wonder exactly how well Lina knew my father. How much she really knows about who I used to be and what I've done.

"Well, Doctor Dent, let's see how well those nerves of steel handle finding us a new ride."

****

Downtown Sonora is a graveyard. The only light on the historic town square comes from the neon sign outside Pinky's Saloon. It's a no-frills bar for the hardcore drinkers, the ones undeterred by Snowmaggedon. The kind of a place with ratty barstools, taxidermy deer heads on the wall, and Willie Nelson playing on the jukebox.

I'll stick out like a sore thumb, which is why I'm grateful to Lina when she tucks her hair into the pink baseball cap, dons her glasses, and sashays toward the old building like she's a regular there. Watching her, I marvel at her self-possession, her confidence. This version of Lina Carr is nothing like my Tuesday 9 a.m. client. I'm not sure which one is real, and that bothers me more than I'd like to admit. Because I can guess how she got this way. How she learned to thicken her skin against the world while her soul cracked beneath it, fragile as a Fabergé egg.

After Lina disappears inside, I slip the burner phone from the go-bag and power it on, searching for a nearby hospital or shopping mall, just as Lina instructed on the ride over. From what I can tell on the phone's mapping application, there's a hospital within five miles where we can abandon my Mini Cooper.

With my task complete, my mind turns to Paige, and I can't resist typing her name into the search bar. The first result knocks the wind out of me like a sucker punch to the gut.

Local Woman Feared Victim Of Foul Play

I scan the article, wincing at the mention of the Obsidian and the Austin Police Department and, finally, of the man I've been for the last seven years.

Psychologist Trevor Dent has been identified as a person of interest. Dent has been missing since this afternoon when police say he was involved in an unusual incident outside the popular store Uncommon Objects, and later at Big Basket grocery store where a man was shot dead. Dent has not been charged with—

The door opens, and I drop the phone to my lap. Lina peers in at me, grinning, sleet falling behind her. In her hand, she jingles a key ring. "Swiped it from his coat when the old guy went in to take a pee. He's so far gone, he'll probably think he forgot where he parked it."

"Which one is it?" I ask.

She presses the lock button on the fob, honking the horn of a blue Ford pickup truck parked a few spots down from Pinky's. "Did you find a spot to dump the Mini?"

I nod, expressionless, though I'm impressed as hell. "Follow me."

CHAPTER 7

SEVEN YEARS EARLIER
TEDDY

Teddy's eyes followed the waitress's perfectly rounded backside as she sashayed toward the kitchen. With so many wannabe actresses looking to make their break, Chateau Marmont had the hottest waitstaff in LA.

"Nice ass, huh?" his father chuckled.

Somehow, Teddy's dad always managed to give voice to the vilest parts of Teddy. The parts he wished he could excise. Horrified, Teddy choked down a sip of water, wishing he could disappear

"I have a girlfriend, Dad."

"You sure do. A real stunner. But you're not dead. Besides, take it from your old man, looking never hurt anyone."

Teddy shifted awkwardly in his seat. It had been two whole weeks since he'd been laid. With Sidney assigned part-time to the Calypso project, he'd barely seen her. And when he had, she'd given him the old headache excuse. Maybe Alan Drucker had a point.

"I'm not sure Tanya would agree with that."

His father smirked, casting off Teddy's challenge like a paper arrow. "I know how to keep a woman happy."

Teddy gritted his teeth behind his smile, fighting the urge to point out that his father had managed to muck up three marriages. That the only person he'd ever managed to keep happy was himself.

"Speaking of keeping people happy . . ." Taking a sip of his dirty martini, Teddy's father sized him up. "Gerry tells me you weren't able to secure the tickets he requested for himself and Senator Crawley?"

"To the Victoria's Secret Fashion Show? It's in London. In three days. And it's been sold out for weeks. Plus, Crawley wanted backstage access. That's virtually impossible." Teddy wanted to add *and none of that's really my job*, but thought better of it.

"Your only job is to keep Gerry happy." Apparently, his dad could read his mind. "Whatever it takes. I don't care if he asks you to bring him a goddamn unicorn. Understand? He's the reason we can afford to eat prime rib at the Marmont for lunch. The downtown expansion project is going to be huge."

When the knockout waitress returned with their appetizers, Teddy kept his eyes on his Caesar salad. His father, meanwhile, stared openly.

"Excuse me, sweetheart. May I just say you should be a model?"

A flush crawled up the young woman's neck, pinking her ears.

Oh God. Teddy thought of crawling beneath the table the way he had at six years old when his father told him his mother wouldn't be living with them anymore. She'd been diagnosed with ALS and needed full-time care. Within a few months, he'd divorced her and banished her to a nursing home, where Teddy had visited her every Saturday with his dad's new girlfriend.

"My law firm represents *Young Chic* magazine. They're already casting for next year's swimsuit issue. It shoots in Bora Bora this spring. If you'd like, I can take your name and number and pass it along. The editor is a personal friend."

His mortification complete, Teddy breathed an audible sigh of relief when his cell buzzed on the table, Sidney's name on the screen. "Excuse me. I have to get this."

Fleeing the restaurant, he pushed through the front door and onto busy Sunset Boulevard. "Hey," he said. "It's not a great time to talk. I'm at lunch downtown at Chateau Marmont. My dad invited some real big wigs." He'd spewed his lies before he could stop them. He wanted to make someone feel the way he did. Unwanted and inept.

"Sorry to bother you." Sidney sounded deflated. She didn't even ask about the big wigs, which made Teddy feel stupid for lying. "But I didn't know who else to call."

"What is it?" he asked, suddenly annoyed with her. With his father. With the whole day.

"It's Mr. Blackstone. He…"

"C'mon, Sid. Spit it out. My steak is getting cold."

He heard the tremble in her breath but said nothing more.

"He's making me uncomfortable. I think he's hitting on me."

CHAPTER 8

WEDNESDAY MORNING
1:45 A.M.
VAN HORN, TEXAS

"Need a break?" Lina asks me, just outside of Van Horn, Texas, another hole-in-the-road town that's taken us three hours to get to.

I'm beginning to think Lina's right. We're stuck in the twilight zone of the Lone Star State, doomed to keep driving toward a perpetual horizon. Already my eyes feel heavy from straining to see through the rain and the sleet and the rock chips that dot the truck's windshield, and I've cracked open the window in an effort to stay awake.

The radio is a lost cause. Nothing but static for forty-five minutes now. But, to be honest, I'm glad. No radio means no news, and I'm not ready to fess up about Paige. Not yet. Maybe not ever.

"I'm fine." I try to sound convincing. At least the truck we pilfered had a full tank of gas and an automatic shift. I haven't driven a stick since my dad caved that once and let me borrow his Porsche 911. "I'll let you take over when we get to El Paso. We should be there in another ninety minutes."

I consult the clock on the dash. 1:45 a.m. Which means truckers and armadillos are the only other live bodies on the road. Across the narrow grassy median, I spot the headlights of a big rig headed east. It zips past us like a comet in the night.

"Suit yourself." She rummages through our haul from the Family Dollar and produces a jumbo bag of Cheetos and a can of Coke. She holds the open bag out to me, tempting me with the aroma of my past. But I shake my head. Trevor doesn't eat processed food.

"I fell asleep for a while." Lina crunches through the first few Cheetos, finishing them off with a swig of soda.

"Yeah. I noticed." Actually, I'd been appalled. After we'd left the Mini in a far corner of the Sutton County General Hospital lot and done another quick plate-swap with a similar Ford truck, Lina had balled her new denim jacket beneath her head and promptly dozed off against the ice-cold window while my heart scampered like a jack rabbit in my chest. "So you steal a lot of cars, then?"

Lina frowns at me and bisects another Cheeto. "I wouldn't say that. But I know how to take what I want without asking. Don't you?"

That question. It's a loaded gun pressed to my chest with her finger on the trigger. And she knows it.

"I'm not like him."

She focuses her eyes on the blacktop ahead—not a soul in sight—and wipes her fingers on her jeans. "Which *him* are you referring to? Gerry Blackstone or your father?"

"Teddy Drucker is who I mean. I'm not that guy anymore. I made a lot of mistakes before I knew better. Surely, you can understand that." The subtle raise of her eyebrows tells me she holds Teddy Drucker against me. I can't say I blame her, but still. I haven't let her down yet. "Is your name really Lina Carr? Is anything you told me about yourself the truth?"

"You're one to talk."

"At least I'm a real psychologist."

"Well, I'm a real head case. With real panic attacks. They started the year I met Gerry."

"How did you meet him?"

"I was introduced. Recruited by a girl a little older than me, at a hotel swimming pool. My mom worked there as a housekeeper, so the manager let me use the pool for free. I laid out every single day, hoping that this cute pool boy, Marco, would notice me. Then Jana offered me a cigarette. Camels."

Lina nudges the Family Dollar bag with her foot and laughs joylessly. "She told me she made extra money giving massages to old, rich guys at the Beverly Wilshire and asked if I wanted to try it. Some were even famous, she said."

"And you agreed to do it?"

"Not at first. But then my mom got laid off from the hotel, and we couldn't afford our rent. I kept sneaking into the pool anyway, and Jana started making eyes at Marco. Of course, she had longer legs and bigger boobs and way more experience, so he was totally into her. One day, I told Jana I'd do it. I wanted to prove something to her."

The sleet turns to snow, soft flakes that collect around the windshield wipers and stick to the glass, nearly obscuring the brake lights in front of me. I slow down, grip the wheel tighter, and maneuver into the left lane to pass a slow-moving SUV. Suddenly, it speeds up, leaving tire tracks on the fresh snow.

"Idiot," I mutter.

Lina hardly notices. "Now I realize it was all a game. A manipulation. She knew I liked Marco, and she used my insecurities against me. But I can't even be mad at her, because one year later, I started doing the exact same thing. I told those girls I'd change their lives."

I let Lina talk. Like I would if we were still in my office on South Congress. It's the most she's ever shared, and it's not lost on me that she's waited until I'm no longer her therapist to start dropping truth bombs.

"The men always got tired of the girls eventually. No matter how pretty you are or how young, they want a new toy to play with. Gerry, most of all. If I planned to keep earning money, I had to make myself irreplaceable." She finally settles her eyes on me. Even the dark cab of the pickup can't hide her shame. "You're not the only one who's done things they're ashamed of."

"You were just a kid trying to survive. What Gerry Blackstone did to you, it's unconscionable."

"It wasn't only Gerry, Trevor."

Every life has a ground zero. A defining moment. As much distance as I put between myself and the past, I remember mine like it happened yesterday. Me yelling. Sidney crying. My cell going off in my pocket, with its ridiculous spy ringtone, and my father on the other end. *Teddy, get down here now. I've been arrested.* Lina's words take me right back there.

"What do you mean?" I ask.

"Watch out!" Lina yells, clutching the bag of Cheetos to her chest.

The same SUV I tried to pass stops hard in the middle of the goddamned road.

I slam the brakes, but the truck resists. It slides forward against my will, faster than I'd expected.

"We're going to hit it." Lina braces for impact, hands against the dash. But I turn the wheel hard to the left, sending us into the grassy median, where the truck comes to a gradual stop, unharmed.

Lina sucks in a ragged breath.

I peer into the rearview for a closer look at the SUV. Black exterior. Texas license plate. The headlights are too bright to make out the figure in the driver's seat. Still, fear dries my mouth and propels me forward. We rumble up off the median and back onto the road.

"Are you alright?" Lina asks.

I nod, not wanting to admit how paranoid I've become. "We need to keep going."

Van Horn flies by in a blur. Two exits and a scattering of city lights give way to barren fields and fence posts that look like crooked figures staggering in the cold dark. My eyes drift repeatedly to the rearview, but all I see is blacktop.

Though Lina resumes her pauper's feast, I can tell she's shaken too. She's eating mindlessly, methodically, as if her life depends on it.

A hard bump from behind jolts me forward, tightening the seat belt against my chest. The Cheetos go flying, scattering across the floorboard. I search the rearview but come up empty. No headlights, only the swirling snow.

"What was that?" Lina looks like a small animal caught in the headlights.

"I can't see any—" Another jarring strike to the bumper, and the truck's wheels start to slide again on the icy road. I turn into the skid slowly until the vehicle is pointed straight. Idling there, I catch my breath.

Suddenly, the bright lights are on us, blaring from behind. Blinding.

"Go!"

At Lina's urging, I punch the accelerator. But the reprieve lasts only a moment before my heart plummets to my knees. The black SUV gives chase, moving into the righthand lane and speeding alongside the truck, dangerously close. The driver's window glides down.

"Gun!"

Lina ducks down, and I punch it again. As we jolt forward, the back wheels fishtail. The SUV eats up ground until we're nose to nose, and it's all I can do to keep the truck on the asphalt.

"They're going to run us off the road." Lina peers up from her crouch, as wide-eyed and terrified as I am. Her face reminds me of Sidney's, the day she disappeared forever.

I have to fix this. I can't let it happen again.

Metal on metal, the SUV knocks against us, and I swerve onto the median, trying to maintain my speed on the rough terrain. The SUV follows, pushing me toward the eastbound lanes. Closer and closer, until I have only two choices. Ram the hell out of it or drive us directly into oncoming traffic.

Suddenly, the glowing eyes of a monster bear down on us. A big rig eating up ground and heading straight for the pickup. It blares its horn like a battle cry.

"Hold on." I brake hard, then yank the wheel to the right, crashing the nose of the pickup against the bumper of the SUV. It skids off into a tailspin before coming to a stop in the muddy grass. By the time I pilot the truck back onto the westbound freeway, the big rig has already roared past and into oblivion.

Glancing in the side mirror, Lina whispers, "Poseidon." As if speaking it out loud might summon them back.

"Did you get a good look at him? Was it—?"

"Derek," she answers.

"At least the snow's let up a little." I search the horizon, desperate for an escape, but find only more wasteland. "We have to get off the road. They're not done with us yet."

Lights reappear from behind. Lina glances over her shoulder, then turns her whole body to the rear of the truck, her voice trembling. "There's someone back there."

"Get the gun." I jerk my head toward the go-bag, resting on the rear floorboard. "Now."

Lina does as she's told, passing the Glock into my hand as I drive. It rests heavy against my thigh. I imagine raising it, aiming it. Pulling the trigger. The one thing Trevor and Teddy have in common, the unyielding will to live. I'll do it if I have to.

"Roll down your window."

The wind rushes in, assaulting me. Clawing at my face with its wet, icy fingers. My eyes tear. My vision blurs. I hold tight to the gun in spite of it or because of it. It gives me a right to feel the rage Trevor Dent keeps swallowing.

Lina whimpers, cowering on the floorboard, as the SUV glides alongside the truck. I feel like Jason Bourne now, waiting for the right time to strike. Looking forward to it, even as my hand shakes.

Through the window, a face blurs in and out of my vision. I squint at it, trying to puzzle the pieces together. The bulbous nose, the receding hairline. The sleazeball smirk I'd know anywhere. My father. I squeeze my eyes shut, open them again. Now it's golden locks and eyes the color of a cloudless day.

"Sidney?"

"Look out!" Lina grabs for the wheel, trying to right our course. But it's too late. The truck careens off the road, takes out two plastic traffic cones, and ends the life of a bush that's grown up in the median.

The SUV pulls off the road ahead of us, its brake lights set upon me like demon eyes. I put the truck in park and fling open the door, armed and prepared to drop anyone who comes near me. Through the sleet, a shadowy figure approaches.

I aim the Glock.

"Easy there, buddy. I don't mean any harm. Just wanted to make sure you're alright."

The gun falls to my side when the stranger steps into the light. He's not Derek Craig. Or my father's ghost. His dirty blond hair falls past his shoulders. His red flannel jacket has a rip in the sleeve. As he backs away, hands raised, I see myself reflected in his eyes. I'm a crazy man.

"We're fine," I say. "Fine."

I white-knuckle it for another ten miles until we reach the Desert Rose Inn. Flannel Man suggested it after Lina flashed a smile—equal parts flirty and apologetic—and told him we needed a break from driving. As if that explained our truck in the ditch and the gun in my hand.

At the front desk, I present the fake ID from my go-bag and secure the last vacant room with an all-cash payment. The Desert Rose is a far cry from the Obsidian. No self-respecting Drucker would be caught dead in a one-star no-tell motel next door to a tire repair shop, which is why I totally dig it.

Though I'm not keen on stopping in the middle-of-nowhere, Texas, with twelve hours to go until Vegas and Paige's life hanging in the balance, I go along. The less Lina knows about Paige the better. She'd get the wrong idea. And the way I've been acting, a few hours of sleep might do me some good.

I drop off Lina in front of Room 33 and park the truck on the other side of the lot, where it won't be seen from the roadway. Upon closer inspection, the front end is a little worse for wear, but it'll get us where we need to go once the storm lets up. Already, the roof of the Desert Rose is covered in a thin layer of white.

Still on high alert, I slide the Glock in my waistband, sling the go-bag over my shoulder, and hurry to the room, nearly slipping a few times on the icy pavement. Lina unlatches the deadbolt and opens the door to our three hundred and twenty-five square feet of relative safety. I collapse onto the bed and release a breath I didn't know I'd been holding.

"You lost it back there." She turns her back to me, tossing the pack of Camels in the trashcan with prejudice. Then she retrieves the scissors and three boxes of hair dye from the plastic bag on the table.

"Can you blame me?" Apparently, she can and does. Her silence says so. "You weren't exactly the picture of calm yourself."

"You called Sidney's name."

I feign confusion. "I did?"

Unfazed and unconvinced, Lina removes the pink baseball cap and gathers her hair into a ponytail, sizing herself up in the full-length mirror on the closet door. It still unnerves me how she resembles Sidney. But then, I'm not surprised. Gerry had a type.

"Want to talk about it?" she asks me.

"Oh, so you're the therapist now?" I prop two lumpy pillows beneath my head and anticipate her smart-ass reply.

"I'll take that as a no, then." In one swift motion, Lina whacks her hair off just below the elastic band. She runs a hand through it, laughing at my astonishment. "Pick your color, Doc. It's time for a change."

Lina rubs my head dry with a towel and wipes the remnants of reddish-brown dye from the sides of the sink basin. It stains the cheap terry cloth the color of dried blood. "It's the best I could do without bleach."

Before I check my new look, I remove my contact lenses, revealing the stormy-blue irises I inherited from my mother. I study the tired face in the mirror. It's part Teddy, part Trevor. "Not bad, not bad."

"My turn." Lina's face appears behind mine in the glass, her eyebrows raised in expectation. She holds a box of chestnut hair color alongside one cheek, raven's black alongside the other.

Either way, she'll be stunning. But I keep that to myself.

"Get out." She places a firm hand on my shoulder and shoves me from the bathroom. There's a smile on her face that doesn't reach her eyes. I realize then that she's rightfully afraid of me. I've got a Y chromosome. I'm a Drucker. And I've proven myself to be unhinged.

The bathroom-door lock clicks into place, confirming my hunch. Resigned, I change my clothes, grateful for the extra boxer briefs I stashed in my go-bag, and scarf down a package of Pop Tarts, another of Lina's dollar-store delicacies. I flop onto the bed and click on the TV, quickly lowering the volume to search for news on Paige. I find nothing but infomercials and reruns. As much as it rattles me, no news is better than a body. Still, Paige is living on borrowed time, and I'm the only one who can do a damn thing about it.

After a few minutes of mindless surfing, I settle on *The Simpsons.* When I can't even manage a laugh at ruthless Mr. Burns twiddling his fingers *à* la Gerry Blackstone, I give up completely and shut my eyes, the sound of the shower drumming like summer rain on a tin roof.

I'm back in my father's garden again, chasing Sidney. Her laughter trails behind her as she flits in between the boxwood topiaries. A flash of her red dress in my periphery leads me toward her hiding place in the hedge maze. That red silk dress, the color of a glass Christmas ornament. It clings to her breasts, skims her thighs. Its hem flutters just north of her knees. I've spent the entire holiday party undressing her with my eyes. I wet my lips. When I find her, she's in big trouble.

"Wake the hell up." The voice isn't Sidney's. That much is certain. Sidney's been gone seven years, and so have I.

My eyes open to a brunette Lina waving the damn gun at me. Her hair is still wet and dripping onto her shirt, leaving two water splotches on her shoulders.

"What the hell is going on?" She gapes at the screen of my burner cell like it's on fire, then tosses it in my direction. "Who is Paige Penny?"

I glance away for a split second, trying to catch a glimpse of what set her off. But she commands my attention with a jab of the barrel into my side. This girl means business, even if her hands are trembling.

"Who is she? What did you do to her?"

"I didn't do anything." I wonder if this is how it ends. Shot dead by my patient. By one of Gerry Blackstone's girls. It would serve me right. "I'll tell you the whole story. Just put the gun down."

"Like hell I will. You have five seconds to start talking." Lina cocks her head at me, daring me to do otherwise.

The cobwebs of sleep razed, I sit bolt upright. "Paige is an escort. She works for Spellbound Services. I've been . . . seeing her for a while now."

"And?" With her non-lethal hand, she nudges the phone toward me. "That doesn't explain this."

"Gordo set me up. I don't know how he did it. But he—"

The headline on the screen stops me cold.

LOCAL PSYCHOLOGIST NAMED AS SUSPECT IN DISAPPEARANCE OF ESCORT, EVIDENCE FOUND AT AUSTIN HOME.

"Evidence?"

"The cops searched your house. They found blood there. Explain that."

I feel sick, imagining Gordo with his slimy hands on my things. This time I really might upchuck. "I can't."

Lina recenters the barrel of the gun so it's looking right at me with its dead eye. "Try."

"I had a date with Paige Monday night at the Obsidian. She was perfectly fine when I left her, I swear. Then I got a call from a guy I assume was Gordo or one of his henchmen. Paige started screaming in the background. He said to deliver the Lolita files to this bridge in LA by Thursday morning."

Finally, she wavers, lowers the Glock to her side. "Los Angeles? I thought I'd never go back there."

"Believe me, I'm not thrilled about it either. But he made it clear what would happen if I didn't. They've done this to me before."

"With Sidney, you mean?"

I hang my head, and the night of the party floods in like a dam burst. Just the way I'd dreamed it. The gardens. The red silk dress. Sidney's lips on mine. *You should be in a movie, Ms. Archer,* Gerry Blackstone had told her, pretending he didn't know what she'd done. He'd offered her a cocktail—while I'd marveled at the nerve of that guy to turn up there, while my father no-showed to his own event, cowering in his room like a frightened puppy.

"Yes, with Sidney."

Lina doesn't look completely convinced, but she sits down, at least, pulling up the well-worn desk chair to face me. She keeps the gun on her lap.

"Blackstone told the cops I was the last one to see her. That he'd watched us leave the party together. That we were arguing. Of course, Gordo backed him up. They even had one of the servers repeat the same story. Probably paid her off."

"I know." Lina blinks up at me, somehow looking innocent and worldly at the same time. "It was me."

"What? You were there that night?" As I try to make sense of it, the walls close in. The room, suddenly as small and airless as a coffin.

"Gerry asked your dad to hire me under the table for the party that night. The catering company wouldn't do it because I was too young, only fifteen. Gerry promised that if I did what he asked, he'd take me to a party like that someday. On his arm. As his date. God, I was such a sucker."

"And what exactly did he ask you to do?"

"Keep an eye on Sidney. Report her movements. She was breathtaking in that red dress."

I can't look away from Lina. Though I'm faltering on the brink of the abyss, I have to say it anyway. "You said you'd tell me what happened to her. You know, don't you?"

My stomach flip-flops while I wait for her mouth to move. To tell me what I already suspect in the deep-down pit of my gut.

"Sidney's dead."

I struggle to swallow the lump in my throat. "How?"

Like an ax through ice, a sharp sound splinters the quiet that follows my question. A gunshot? It must be. On instinct, I drop to the ground, tugging Lina with me.

"What was that?" she whispers.

Already I'm belly-crawling toward the window's edge, peering around the opening in the blinds. Through the sleet storm, I spot a pair of headlights. The body of a hot rod. The driver revs the engine, causing another backfire, and the vehicle rumbles past the room and out of the lot, disappearing into the early morning.

"It's just some jackass spinning his wheels. The coast is clear." I stand up and start pacing, disgusted by how easily I've let the monsters from my past take hold.

Lina stays on the floor, sitting cross-legged.

"So what were you saying?" I ask. Sidney's red dress ripples at the edges of my imagination, bleeds into my concentration. I bite the inside of my lip to stay focused.

"The Lolita files aren't just *files.* If they went so far as to kidnap Paige, there's something else they want." She reaches for the burner phone, her fingers stabbing at the screen without mercy. Then, saying nothing, she holds it out to me.

I snatch it from her hand as if it's on fire, and it might as well be. Incredulous, I shake my head, trying to convince myself. "There's no such thing. It's an urban legend." Still, I read the rest of the words anyway, straight from the internet, the place where fact and fiction live side by side as reluctant neighbors.

A snuff film is a pornographic video which depicts scenes of an actual homicide. The term originated in the 1970s with a low-budget pornographic movie titled "Snuff," which rose to notoriety when its distributor attempted to drum up publicity by inciting women's groups to protest the film under the false impression that it showed an actual murder. Though some claim that snuff films are genuine, experts who work for the FBI and other law enforcement agencies maintain that the majority of these films are realistic fakes and that pornographic material depicting the actual homicide of human beings likely does not exist.

"You're saying there's a snuff film in my dad's secret files? Do you know how crazy that sounds?"

"Think what you want, but it's real." She lowers her voice like she's afraid someone is listening. "I've seen it."

CHAPTER 9

SEVEN YEARS EARLIER
SIDNEY

Sidney returned to her temporary office at the Calypso Development Group, locking the door behind her. She felt silly, stupid. She should've have kept her mouth shut. She should've known Teddy would hold the party line.

Don't make a big deal of it, Sid. Gerry's a touchy-feely kind of guy. Harmless. Besides, we need him. My career depends on it. And so does yours.

She supposed it had started innocently enough. A pat on the shoulder while she worked overtime, drafting applications for business permits. An accidental bump of his knee beneath the conference table. A wink and a gaze that lingered too long. No stranger to men who couldn't take a hint, Sidney had done her best to ignore him, to play defense. Even now, she wore her armor. A turtleneck, long slacks, and the most boring flats she owned. Not a smidge of makeup on her face.

She took out her phone and studied Blackstone's text again, second-guessing herself. Maybe she had overreacted.

I won't be in today. Could you bring a copy of the purchase agreements to my hotel room for review? I promise to behave.

Just get it over with, she coached herself, pretending to be Teddy. It's the middle of the day, Sid. You can talk your way out of anything. Gathering the files Blackstone requested, she ignored the violent protests of her stomach and typed *Beverly Wilshire Hotel* into her phone's mapping application.

****

Sidney scored a parking spot a few blocks from the four-star hotel, deciding a walk might clear her head. Psych her up to get through this. When she arrived at the lobby, she found a quiet spot and texted Blackstone, hoping he'd agree to come down to meet her instead.

Once she'd asked one of the Calypso paralegals why he stayed at a hotel instead of at his lavish home in the Hollywood Hills. The middle-aged woman had laughed at her. *Closer to the action,* she'd said, rolling her eyes.

The buzz of Sidney's phone startled her.

Still getting ready. Come up. I'm in the Penthouse Suite. Fourteenth Floor.

Without reply, she trudged on leaden legs toward the elevator, dreading the ding that signaled her arrival. At the door to the suite, she barely tapped the bell, half hoping he wouldn't hear her. She thought of dropping the files out front and hightailing it out of there. But she knew what that would mean. Leaving confidential client information unsecured would be sure grounds for termination. And with that on her record, she could kiss USC goodbye.

When the door opened, Sidney nearly gasped. A girl stood there, wearing a plush bathrobe and white slippers embroidered with the hotel's logo. She reminded Sidney of herself as a teen, face scrubbed fresh with sun-kissed highlights in her wet blonde hair.

"Oh, I'm sorry. I must have the wrong room."

"Come in, Ms. Archer." Blackstone's voice traveled from somewhere inside the expansive suite.

Reluctantly, Sidney stepped into the opulent foyer as the girl sashayed down the hall and disappeared behind a door. Moments later, Blackstone emerged in his bathrobe, the tie dangerously slack at his waist.

"Was that your daughter?" His slimy grin made Sidney curse herself for asking.

"Something like that. You can think of her as my assistant if you'd like."

Sidney frowned but kept her mouth shut.

"Did you bring the files?"

She'd nearly forgotten why she'd come. Sliding the folder from her purse, she took the chance to back away from him and laid the papers on the glass coffee table. "Anything else?"

"Don't rush off so soon. Sit down. Have a drink with me." Blackstone gestured to the bar, where he'd already set out two glasses and a bottle of white wine, assuming she would say yes. A kernel of rage hardened inside her. "Let's talk about your future. I hear great things about the work you've been doing on the development. Alan tells me you want to go to law school. Possibly USC."

Sidney nodded, not sure where to put her eyes. Blackstone's robe loosened as he moved toward the bar, flashing his obscenely white thigh peppered with wiry black hair.

"That's a highly ranked institution. I completed my undergraduate degree there, as I'm sure you're aware. My recommendation will go a long way. I assume you'll be wanting one." By the time he poured his glass to the brim and raised it to her, the front of the robe gaped open, leaving him fully exposed. "Perhaps I could even arrange a private meeting with the dean."

"I really should go. There's so much to do back at the office. I want to pull my weight."

Blackstone cocked his head at her. "How much *do* you weigh?"

"Excuse me?"

"Your measurements? I know a lot of the top designers. They could make you a one-of-a-kind gown for the firm's holiday party. Maybe something red." He paused, then stepped toward her, his eyes squarely on her chest. "What are you, a C cup? Dress size 6?"

Sidney wanted to run. She wanted to slap him. To tell him to go fuck himself. But she found that none of the things she wanted to do got done. Instead, she froze, stuck in the middle of the Penthouse Suite, no more able to move than the crystal vase on the credenza.

"I didn't mean to embarrass you." Mercifully, he closed his robe, cinching it at his midsection. "Sometimes, I can be too forward. If I've gone too far, just pretend it never happened."

Sidney saw the girl watching them coolly from the far corner of the room. At a distance, she had an air of sophistication that made Sidney wonder if she'd misjudged her age. Misjudged this alien world she'd stumbled into. Still, she worried for the girl, wishing she could get her alone.

"C'mon, Gerry," the girl said. "Don't you have a two o'clock appointment with the senator? He'll be here any minute."

Blackstone pretended not to hear her for a moment. Then he nodded. "Coming." And to Sidney, he asked, almost as an afterthought, "A rain check on that drink?"

She gulped down a wicked cocktail of disgust and relief, certain she would've said anything to get out of that room. "Sure."

Sidney burst out the door to Blackstone's suite, desperate to be free of him. He hadn't touched her, yet her skin crawled. She was in need of a good scrubbing beneath a scalding hot shower.

Trying to recover, she raised her eyes a breath too late, running straight into the man in front of her.

"Senator Crawley, I'm so sorry." She recognized him from the celebratory election-day photo in Blackstone's office. Word around the office was the senator and Gerry had attended USC together. Both members of Kappa Sig.

Crawley flashed her that same victory smile she'd seen in the frame. "Are you alright, my dear? You seem troubled. I hope Gerry hasn't upset you. Or he'll have to answer to me."

"I'm okay." Sidney fixed herself, straightening her blouse. Her cheeks felt hot with the tears she'd been holding back. She sniffled. "But what about you? Clumsy me, I practically mowed you down."

"Good thing I'm no pushover." Crawley chuckled, flexing his small bicep, barely visible beneath his button down. "Do you work for Calypso? I haven't seen you before."

"Drucker and Webber, sir. But I'm just a paralegal." Regaining her composure, Sidney realized how rude she'd been. "I should've introduced myself. Sidney Archer."

He gave her hand a polite squeeze. "Not *just* a paralegal. Don't ever sell yourself short. If you ask me, paralegals do all the hard work to make us attorneys look good."

When she heard movement behind Blackstone's door, Sidney's laugh stuck in her throat. "If you'll excuse me, I have to get back to the office. It was a pleasure to meet you."

"You as well, Ms. Archer. I do hope we meet again."

As she booked it to the elevator, the door to the suite opened behind her, but she didn't dare look back.

CHAPTER 10

WEDNESDAY MORNING
4 A.M.
DESERT ROSE INN

From the bed I've made on the floor of Room 33, I watch Lina warily, afraid of waking up with a gun to my vital bits. I consider leaving her here, slipping out under the cover of darkness and hightailing it to Vegas on my own. But as far as I can tell, she's not sleeping either.

Beneath the grumbling of the wall-mounted heater, I listen hard for her breathing, waiting for the rhythmic push and pull, the cadence of deep sleep. But it never comes. And every time I open my eyes, Lina's are looking right back, glinting in the eerie glow of the alarm clock.

At 4 a.m., I relent, pushing myself up from the cheap carpet and padding to the bathroom with the care of a cat burglar. Lina doesn't move, but I'm not fooled. I splash my face with ice-cold water, run a hand through my hair, and squirt a dab of Family Dollar toothpaste onto my finger, amused by my vanity.

When I nudge open the door, Lina is sitting on the bed, dressed and waiting.

"We should go," she says.

I nod my agreement. Though I don't need her, she needs me, and it's nice to be needed after going it alone all this time. Besides, the thought of sticking a knife in Blackstone's back sounds like the kind of therapy that will set us both right again.

We pack our things in silence and stand side by side in front of the door, solemn as soldiers before a battle. Taking no chances, I hold the gun in my hand as I unlatch the deadbolt and take the first step.

Overnight, the storm left its mark on the world. Blown about by the heavy wind, branches lay like bodies, dotting the thin layer of snow that will melt to slush once the sun rises. But right now, in the glow of the pole lights, the Desert Rose is serene. A blank canvas that nearly convinces me things will turn out alright.

Until I spot the black SUV parked outside room 33, its front end facing our door. A large dent mars the side panel. Ice covers the windshield, making it impossible to see inside.

I stumble backward, knocking into Lina, her face gone ghost-white. She points at the driver's window, the glass splintered by a bullet hole. Paralyzed by fear, I stare at it for a heartbeat before we both book it back inside, slamming the door behind us.

"What the hell?" I inch back the blinds and peer out at the parking lot. Nothing stirs. Even the wind dies, leaving the place pin-drop quiet.

"That's the Poseidon SUV." Lina stands behind me, looking out over my shoulder. "Do you think Derek is still in there?"

"Only one way to find out."

"I'm coming with you. We're in this together now."

I don't argue, because the truth is I'm scared as hell. I'm not a Drucker. I don't call the shots anymore. Now I'm a nobody. I'm just the little man getting taken for a ride.

I drop my duffel on the sidewalk and approach the SUV, my eyes darting from one end of the lot to the other. I hold the gun close, finger on the trigger, hoping I won't get bested by another baldie dead set on trying to end my life. Frost covers the spider cracks in the driver's window, so I lean down and squint through the jagged hole.

A man, slumped over the console. His skin, an unnatural hue.

"It's Derek," I mutter.

Blood tracks down his face from a single, perfect wound in his temple. The metallic smell of it, unmistakable. I follow the trail to his chest. To the note pinned there—with my name on it—beneath the small gold trident.

I pull back, taking in a breath of biting-cold air as if it's my last.

"What is it?" Lina asks.

"I'm not sure. But I need to get inside. Keep a look out." Passing the gun to Lina, I glance over my shoulder once more, then stretch the sleeve of my sweatshirt to cover my hand, gingerly opening the door.

Lina stands frozen, on high alert. Like a deer in the woods caught in the hunter's sights.

I channel what's left of the old me, the former master of self-deception. Because I desperately need to convince myself that I'm not touching the blood-soaked shirt of a dead man. Careful not to leave any prints, I work the safety pin open and remove the piece of paper addressed to me. I read the words fast, then crumple it and shove it into my pocket before Lina can see it.

"Let's get the hell out of here."

Lina stays rooted to the spot until I seize her by the arm, pulling her along with me as I grab my bag and bolt for the truck.

With Lina finally moving behind me, I fling open the door and climb inside, already turning the key. The sound of the straining engine sinks my heart to the bottom of my stomach. Despairing, I turn the key again—with the need to run like hell more powerful than ever.

Derek's a goner. I saw it with my own eyes. But in my mind he's lumbering behind us, undead, and leaving a trail of his blood in the snow.

"C'mon," I growl, giving the key another sharp yank.

Finally, the engine roars to life, and I pump my fist in the air as if I've just thrown a touchdown pass. Lina cheers too, then laughs. By the time we've reached the interstate on-ramp, we're both breathless with the kind of giddiness that comes from the sheer relief of survival.

"Do you think Gordo killed him?" Lina asks, glancing in the side mirror. Like she still can't quite believe we made it out alive.

That makes two of us.

"That's my hunch. Gordo wants those files. He's never been good at sharing."

"Do you believe me now? About the film?"

As I gaze down the lonesome stretch of road, I feel her search my face.

"Blackstone knows there's something in those files worth killing for," she says.

I'm glad it's still dark. Lina can't see me shiver.

When she falls asleep in the passenger seat twenty minutes later, her head lolling against the window, I fish the note out of my pocket and read it once more:

Trevor—

Don't be late. You know what's at stake.

P.S. Come alone. Loose ends will need cutting.

Loose ends. Those words come straight from Gordo's mouth, straight from the past. They careen through my head like a stray bullet. I crack open the driver's window and watch the note take flight. Whipped by the wind and buried in the wet snow, it's gone in an instant. But I know what it means. If I don't get rid of Lina, Gordo will do it for me.

****

Tell me about Sidney." Lina's voice startles me.

While she slept, I grew accustomed to the hum of the highway, the drone of the truck's engine. The quiet chatter of talk radio that drowned the whispers of the past. Now she's summoned it front and center.

"What do you want to know?"

"Did you love her?"

Right for the jugular. "I thought I did. But, looking back, I don't believe I was capable. I just didn't want anyone else to have her." I grip the wheel tighter, recalling the feel of Sidney's hand on my arm as I led her into my father's holiday party. Heads turned, and I got a rise out of it. She'd chosen me out of all the Ivy League chumps. I felt like a winner with a championship trophy to kiss for the cameras.

"I'm not surprised," Lina says. "You didn't have the best role model in that department."

"You mean marrying four women isn't normal?" A laugh, one-note, clunks from my throat. "What about you? Did your mom know what was going on with Blackstone?"

Lina twists her mouth, the same way she'd done in our sessions anytime I'd asked about her childhood. The shrink in me wonders what she's working so hard to hold back. I want to coax it out of her even though I don't have the right.

"My mom never got married. But that didn't stop her from letting a revolving door of guys beat the hell out of her. I used to ask myself why she always picked the losers. Then I realized they picked her, and she never demanded better. I'd rather die than end up like that."

"And one of those losers was your dad?"

She gives me a sad smile, and I wonder if it's easier to lay herself bare in the dark. "Probably. I never knew him. Every time I asked my mom, she'd tell me something different. He was an airline pilot. A marine. He played for the Dodgers. Finally, she got really drunk one night and told me the truth. She had no freaking clue which loser got her pregnant. Anyway, she's gone now. Lung cancer."

"I'm sorry. It sounds like we both drew the short straw when it comes to parental units."

Lina reaches into the back pocket of her jeans and pulls out a photo, the paper soft and worn. The woman poses on Rodeo Drive, an older version of Lina, flirting with the camera, sharing a secret through her smile. "She was beautiful though, right? Your dad would've liked her."

"I'm sure he would have." Strange, but I think of my mother, wiping her tears in the microwave's reflection after my father had been gone all night. "Liked her enough to cheat on her. My dad treated his wives—and his only son—like anything else he owned. He paid to keep us. We were all replaceable."

After a long silence, Lina shakes her head at me and launches a poison arrow. "I don't get it, Trevor."

"Get what?" Though I can guess what she's hinting at, and I don't like it. Because it comes with the sting of self-hatred.

"You said you were nothing like him or Gerry. But Paige is an escort. Kind of hypocritical, don't you think?"

The first time I'd called Spellbound Services I'd been living in Austin for four years. Celibate as a priest and intent on staying that way. Until the dreams started. Sidney in the garden in the red dress. I'd wake up sweating through my T-shirt and inexplicably turned on. After a month of that kind of torture, a one-night stand with a call girl seemed like the least of my problems.

"She wasn't just another escort," I tell Lina. "She was the only one."

"So you paid your girlfriend for sex so you wouldn't get too attached. Is that about the size of it?"

I shrug, glad the sun hasn't shown its face yet. I can still hide in the thin light of the dawn.

"Sheesh. Are you sure you're qualified to be dishing out advice?"

"Unfortunately, having a doctorate degree doesn't mean you're an expert in your own shit."

I'm grateful when Lina tables the discussion and points to the lights on the horizon instead. Like the swayed backs of sleeping giants, the Franklin Mountains rise behind the El Paso skyline. We both stare in disbelief. Finally, we've reached the western-most end of Texas.

I stop to fill up at the next exit, selecting the most rundown gas station I can find. The single pump outside Moe's Gas & Snacks seems our best bet to avoid any pesky security cameras. Now that I'm my *new* old self again, I ditch my ball cap on the seat and hop out into the frigid morning.

"Hungry?" Lina asks, her eyes focused on Rosita's Cantina, a neon-pink eyesore with a full parking lot and an inflatable sombrero atop the roof. The sign out front promises the biggest breakfast burritos in Texas.

I peel off a twenty and watch Lina dart across the access road and disappear inside the stucco building. For a heartbeat, I imagine myself leaving her behind, peeling out in a cloud of exhaust. Gordo has spoken, and he's not a patient man. Instinctively, my eyes search the periphery, peering into the shadows. The only sign of life, a black cat darting through a hole in the fence.

I hurry inside, planning to drop two more twenties on the counter and mutter a *thanks* to the bleary-eyed woman behind it. But the line is three deep. By the time I return to top off the tank, Lina has beaten me back. She's seated in the cab, the smell of eggs and chorizo wafting from the paper bag in her hand. What I'd give to go back to my last real meal. Dinner with Paige on Monday night. If I'd known then, I would've told Paige the truth. That I'd fallen for her. I would've taken her somewhere far from Austin. Just hopped in the Mini and kept driving until the sun rose. But that's a pipe dream now.

"Check this out." Lina brings me right back to our unreality, handing me a folded sheet from her pocket. A violent rip at the top center of the paper tells me she snagged it from a bulletin board. "I think I found us a new ride."

SE VENDE CARRO

1980 CHEVY IMPALA

$1500

Scrawled beneath the handwritten advertisement is a phone number.

"I don't know. It sounds like a beater." I toss the paper onto the seat and reach into the bag. Watching Lina peel back the foil from her burrito, I'm suddenly ravenous. "Besides, we should stay on the road. We still have ten hours to Vegas, and I'm not even sure what the hell we're looking for."

Lina groans before taking an enthusiastic bite. "It won't hurt to call. Poseidon is going to send some new creeps after us, and I guarantee they'll be looking for a blue Ford pickup."

As much as I'd rather focus on scarfing down breakfast, I know she's right. "Fine. We'll dial the number. But if it's too far out of our way, I say we keep trucking."

Ten minutes later, I already have massive regrets. We're somewhere on the outskirts of El Paso taking directions over the burner phone in broken English from a man called Loco. The farther south we drive, the more ramshackle the houses become, some of them abandoned entirely, with plyboard windows and yards dotted with trash. Graffiti marks the fences like war paint, and I keep one hand on the Glock at my waist.

"There." Lina points to the dead end of the street where a man stands waving to us, a small dog yipping at his side.

Though the sun has finally breached the horizon, I can't quite make out his face beneath the hood of his jacket. But he moves like a rusted tinman, his steps stuttering. Loco, I presume.

"Are you sure about this?" I ask her, slowing the truck to a crawl. "It looks like a good place to get jacked."

"If they want to meet the bad end of my stun gun." Lina shrugs me off as she rolls down her window, calling to the man. He ushers us toward the house on his left, muttering in Spanish.

I park alongside the driveway, scanning the place for signs of an ambush. Like the indistinguishable face that appears between the curtains, then disappears, letting them fall back into place across the barred window. But there's a harmless pink tricycle on the porch with handlebar streamers. And the Impala is real, sitting toward the back of the yard, frost coating the windshield. It's been repainted a shade of seasick green.

"Fifteen hundred for that?" I hiss at Lina. "At least let me handle the negotiation. I know business." Never mind that as Senior Client Relations Manager, I'd been more interested in kissing ass than driving a hard bargain. The best deal I ever negotiated involved getting my officemate, Nick, to cover for my slacker ass in exchange for courtside seats to the Lakers.

Lina cocks her head at me, unsmiling. "So do I."

The old man disappears inside the house, leaving the little dog yipping anxiously at the door. When it opens again, a woman scoops up the dog, cradling it like a baby. In her bathrobe and fur-lined boots, she looks tragically comic. *She's got a few miles on her,* my father would have said. Her hair, dark as crow's feathers, is piled atop her head in a messy bun, and a cigarette dangles precariously from her lips. I wonder how many holes she's burned in that robe.

I crack the truck's door, reminding myself we've come this far. And I have no desire to see Poseidon on our tail again. Still uncertain, I slide the Glock into my waistband and wait.

Lina makes her way to the Impala and around it, kicking the tires before giving me a thumbs up.

The woman looks right at me, before she tosses her cigarette onto the wet ground, tamping it with her toe, and joins Lina in the yard. She sets the dog onto the grass, but he stays close, jumping at her feet.

"*Buenas dias.* You the girl who called about the car?"

"Yep." At least Lina didn't tell her our names. "Can we start it up?"

"Runs like a jackrabbit. I fixed it myself. It'll get you where you need to go."

"No offense, but I need to test the merchandise."

Reaching into the pocket of her robe, the woman removes a set of keys. She works one from the ring and passes it to Lina.

"No test drives," she says. "Cash only."

Lina nods as she takes a seat inside the Impala and cranks the engine. It roars to life, sounding better than I'd anticipated on a cold morning like this one. "Twelve fifty and not a penny more," Lina counters. "The right front tire is practically bald. And I doubt you'll get a better offer from the patrons at Rosita's."

"Might be right. But you seem hard up for a ride, coming all the way out here at daybreak." For the first time, the woman addresses me, meeting my eyes across the yard. I want to look away but don't. "Your truck got a body in it or something?"

Last night comes back in a flash. The truck careening off the road. The man I almost shot dead. The running tally of bodies we've left behind us—that I've left behind *me.* I can't blame Lina for any of this.

"Take it or leave it," Lina says, exiting the Impala. Depositing the key on the hood, she saunters toward me without looking back.

When she's reached the truck, the woman calls out to her.

"Wait." She picks up the dog, fending off his licking tongue, and trudges after Lina. "You got yourself a deal. I'm glad to be rid of it anyway."

"Why's that?" I ask her, finally pushing the door wide and emerging from the warm cocoon of the truck. I leave it running.

"It belonged to my ex. He dumped me for some *puta* he met at a swap meet."

"I'm sorry."

"Don't be. Let that bastard beat up on some other broad for a while. Besides, he left the best damn part of him behind. Didn't he, Diego?" She cuddles the chihuahua.

Lina smiles at the little dog, looking brighter than I've ever seen her. "Can I pet him?"

"You can hold him if you want. But he's a biter."

My eyes travel from Lina to the Impala to the go-bag and back again. I think of all she's been through. Gordo's warning sinks its claws into me, drawing blood, until I have no choice. Lina's best chance is to stay as far away from me as possible, even if it means I've got to go it alone.

Without a word, I hoist myself back into the driver's seat and shut the door. I jerk the truck in drive and peel out, leaving Lina behind. Though I hear her yelling after me, I don't look back. But I imagine her anyway, standing there shell-shocked with Diego in her arms.

CHAPTER 11

WEDNESDAY AFTERNOON
1 P.M.
PHOENIX, ARIZONA

I spend the next six hours trying not to think. Trying to shut off the part of my brain that earned a degree in clinical psychology. The part that knows denial isn't healthy, that compartmentalization is not a coping skill. That the empty seat beside me means I left Lina in the middle of nowhere, El Paso with no money, no car, and no explanation.

Better that than Gordo's bullet in her head, though. I did the right thing. That's what I tell myself as the old truck eats the blacktop and the road signs fly by in a blur. The scenery changes, the weather too. Too bad I'm the same sorry sucker I've always been. Turns out you can change your name, your hair, even the goddamn color of your eyes, but beneath it all, you're still you. For better or worse.

Somewhere between Tucson and Phoenix, one rogue thought slips through my defenses, and all hell breaks loose. One realization at a time.

Sidney is dead.

Paige has been kidnapped.

The cops are looking for me.

They found blood in my house.

And it's all my fault.

I follow the directions on the burner cell to a strip mall outside of Phoenix. Sure enough, near the entrance to the Fashion Factory clothing store, there's an old-school payphone, just like the website promised. After a quick surveil reveals no visible cameras, I park at the edge of the lot for a quick getaway and rustle up a few quarters to make a call I'll probably regret.

No surprise, Detective Vega answers on the first ring. "Candace Vega, Homicide."

A chill runs through me. I nearly hang up.

"Hello? Is anyone there?"

I hear myself swallow. I wish I'd shed the sweatshirt in the truck. The sun feels like a spotlight on my face.

"It's me. Trevor. Trevor Dent."

"Trevor. I'm glad you called." She's smooth under pressure. Smoother than I could ever hope to be. I picture her at the station, waving to her turkey-necked partner with one hand while she placates me through the phone she's holding in the other. "I was worried for your safety. Where are you?"

"I saw the news report about the blood. I know it looks bad, but I didn't do anything wrong. I swear I'd never hurt Paige."

"Even if you did, Trevor, you must have had a good reason. There's a lot going on in your life right now. Couples fight. Things happen."

I know exactly what Detective Vega is doing. She's not the first cop to try it. Back in LA, it was the same story. *You must've been angry with Sidney for going to the cops. She put your father in jail and his best client too. That would be enough to make me go ballistic. Maybe things got out of hand, went farther than you intended.*

"I'm telling you I'm innocent. Someone's setting me up. I can't say any more than that." My eyes dart through the parking lot, half expecting a cop car to screech up to the booth. Or worse, new goons from Poseidon. Worst of all, Gordo himself. "I've gotta go. It's not safe. I know you're tracing this call." The receiver trembles in my hand, and I grip it tighter. It has a life of its own now. It wants me to keep talking, to tell her everything.

"Wait. Don't hang up. Trevor?"

I freeze, the receiver inches from the cradle. I can hear her breathing. I wipe the sweat from my forehead.

"We found the knife."

A strangled sound croaks out of me, while my thoughts rush by, faster than those signs on the highway.

"In the air-conditioning vent. It's covered in Paige Penny's blood. Her mother gave a DNA sample for comparison."

I've watched enough true crime documentaries to doubt her, even as my lungs squeeze shut. DNA takes weeks, months. Years even. And I felt certain Paige had slipped once and told me that her mom died years ago. Spellbound had rules about that. No personal information. Yet I knew Paige's body like she'd drawn me a map. Her sounds, her smiles. Her perfect imperfections.

The irony smacks me in the face. Hard. And I finally manage to speak. "I can't make the same mistake twice. I'm going to save Paige. Please don't try to stop me." I slam the phone onto the hook in a panic. Then I hurry back to the truck, forcing myself not to run. I strip off the sweatshirt and toss it in the back seat, near the go-bag. The zipper is partly undone, half the bag gaping open like a smirking mouth.

I try to remember when I saw it last. At the gas station in El Paso, before I'd gone inside to pay. Lina had returned before me.

Unleashing a string of curse words, I haul the bag onto the passenger seat and tug the zipper the rest of the way. My relief lasts only long enough for me to catalog the contents. Lina left me the laptop, the falsified documents, and most of the money. I empty the bag, shaking it out onto the floorboard. Empty.

There's no sign of the chain Alan Drucker wore around his neck. The same chain I collected from the hospital morgue the day he died—the chain I contemplated giving to a homeless man on Hollywood Boulevard just for the hell of it. Hopeless, I look again, running my hand inside the interior of the cheap duffel.

Except for the overpriced watches he collected like baseball cards, my father never wore jewelry. Couldn't even be bothered with a wedding ring. So when he showed up at the office that December with an antique-finished chain glinting beneath his collar, I'd taken notice. Then in the gym sauna after work, I'd spotted it again. The strangely shaped pendant nestled perversely among his salt-and-pepper chest hair. Its obnoxious row of precious stones—ruby and black jade—winking at me.

What's that? I'd asked him, staring down at my chest, still sore from Bruce's maniacal push-up routine.

He'd touched the chain carefully before answering. *Just something I picked up in Vegas.*

His last earthly possession. And now Lina has it. I didn't expect to care, but the loss of it twists my gut. I wonder if she'll pawn it for a ride or fasten it around her neck, smug in her victory.

As I tear down the freeway—four hours to Vegas—I have to admit it. I'm a lousy shrink. Because even after two months of therapy, I don't know Lina Carr. I don't know her at all.

CHAPTER 12

SEVEN YEARS EARLIER
SIDNEY

Sidney ignored her mother's call for the third time that week. She didn't know what to say. How to explain the mess she'd found herself in. How to admit she couldn't grin and bear it anymore.

If she tried to lie, her mom would see right through her. But telling the truth would be worse, because she'd be forced to concede defeat. To crawl away with her tail tucked between her legs, wondering if she could ever hack it as the badass attorney she wanted to be.

Her parents had already proclaimed her move to LA a mistake. And when she'd told them about Teddy and his magazine cover, her father had warned her. *The deeper the pockets, the colder the soul.* Neither of them had ever left small-town Kernville. What could they possibly understand about the world she lived in now?

Since that afternoon at the Beverly Wilshire when she'd found Blackstone and his young assistant in their bathrobes,

Hurricane Gerry had grown bigger and stronger, eclipsing her world in a dark cloud. Her stellar performance evaluation didn't help matters. Because now Alan Drucker had assigned her full-time to the Calypso account, which meant late-night meetings and dinners and constant unwanted attention.

Even Blackstone's business trip to New York didn't stop his steady stream of texts well into the wee hours of the morning. After she'd turned him down on that rain check, he'd flipped his script overnight, going from creepy pervert to demanding asshole.

After listening to her mother's message—*Are you okay, honey? Call me. Your father and I are worried about you.*—Sidney returned to the strange folder she'd discovered misfiled with the site plans. Opening it again, she scrutinized the list of cash deposits. Each had been wired to an offshore account owned by Erinnyes, an apparent Calypso subsidiary with cash holdings in excess of ten million dollars. As far as she could tell, the payments were unaccounted for in Calypso's financial records.

Taking a breath, Sidney dialed Alan Drucker, chewing on her bottom lip as the phone rang. When he finally answered, he sounded the way he always did. Too busy to be bothered.

"Hello, Mr. Drucker, it's Sidney. I'm sorry to bother you, but—"

"What is it?"

"As you know, I've been drafting the applications for the building permits with the help of Mr. Blackstone's assistant, Marsha. She provided me with the site plans and—"

"Cut to the chase, Ms. Archer. I have a two-thirty client meeting."

"Have you heard of Erinnyes?" She stumbled a bit over the word. Thanks to Google, she knew it had meaning: the three Greek goddesses of vengeance who punished men for their crimes against the natural order. "It's a Calypso subsidiary."

"Erinnyes?" he repeated.

"Over the last few years, there were a number of large cash deposits made to that account at the Bank of Grand Cayman. I thought it would be prudent to bring it to your attention."

"Where's the file now?"

"Right here on my desk."

"Return it to Marsha immediately. I'll have a talk with Gerry later." After a long pause, he added, "I expect you'll be discreet."

"Of course, but—"

He'd already hung up.

Sidney gathered the financials, a cold unease settling into her bones. Before she could talk herself out of it, she snapped photos of the pages with her cell. Then she made the short walk to Blackstone's office and laid the file in Marsha's in-box.

"This was mixed up with the site plans."

Marsha glared at her as if she'd levied an insult.

"I didn't look at it." Her lie hung in the air between them, until Marsha dismissed her with a wave of her manicured hand.

Scurrying away from Marsha's evil eye, Sidney retreated to her desk, but she couldn't focus with the chatter in her head. At three o'clock, she decided she deserved a break. With Blackstone gone, she could head home early, go for a long run, take a bubble bath. Something to clear the storm that had rolled in, threatening to drown her.

When she pushed through the double doors and onto the sidewalk, she stopped cold.

"Teddy?"

"Hey, beautiful." Like it hadn't been a week since they'd talked. Like he could still charm her into anything. "I came looking for you. We need to chat."

"About what?"

Teddy pointed down the street to the little coffee shop on the corner. "Their chocolate scones will change your life. We can talk inside."

Sidney followed Teddy in silence. She had the strange feeling she'd done something wrong. That she was about to be scolded. But then he took her by the hand, giving her fingers a little squeeze as they walked.

"My dad is worried about you. I told him you're fine, but he insisted I come and see you in person." One corner of his mouth turned up. "Okay, okay. I might've had my reasons too. I miss you."

His smile tugged at her heartstrings—*God, she was pathetic*—and she stopped to face him. "I miss you too. I've been so busy on the Calypso account. I barely have time to breathe. And—"

"Dad said you found an anomaly in the financials."

Sidney hesitated. "Yeah, I suppose. Between you and me, Erinnyes looks like a shell company. But that's not the real problem. Mr. Blackstone is . . ." Sidney searched for the right word that would make him believe her. That would make him take her side this time. "He's not very professional. Do you think you could ask your dad to reassign me? I don't want to work with him anymore."

Teddy scrunched his face in confusion. "I don't get it, Sid. Gerry sings your praises. He told my dad to double your pay. What gives? Did you sleep with him?"

"What?"

"Sorry. You're just acting weird. And you've been avoiding me. I thought maybe something happened between the two of you. He can be really convincing, and he has a thing for blondes. I know he likes you."

Sidney dropped Teddy's hand and steadied herself against the outside wall of the coffee shop, trying not to cry. "That's why he asked for me in the first place, isn't it?"

Teddy squirmed, didn't answer.

Lowering her voice, Sidney leaned in, tears filming her eyes. "He's been sexually harassing me. There's no way to sugarcoat it."

"Whoa, whoa, whoa. Keep your voice down." Teddy's eyes darted down the empty sidewalk. "That's a loaded accusation. Don't blow it out of proportion. Remember, he's my dad's best client."

She hadn't planned on spilling her guts, but now that she'd started, she couldn't stop. She wanted to shock him. "Last week, he told me I reminded him of his first."

"First . . . paralegal?"

"*Sexual partner.*" Teddy could be so dense sometimes.

"Geez, Sid. Are you sure that's how he meant it?"

"How else could he mean it? Best client or not, he's a creep, Teddy."

"Okay, okay. Let me talk to Dad. He'll know what to do. He always does." He gave her hand a tug, leading her inside. Flashed her his roguish grin. "Until then, let's eat."

CHAPTER 13

WEDNESDAY AFTERNOON
2:30 P.M.
LAS VEGAS, NEVADA

Las Vegas is a Rorschach inkblot. People see what they want in those bright lights. Take Gerald Blackstone, for example. Gerry never met a craps table he didn't like. Always a beautiful, young woman on his arm who'd softly blow on those red dice before he let them fly, then whoop when the die landed on lucky seven.

My father preferred a more subtle game, sipping his Macallan 18 in the high rollers' blackjack pit. Teddy Drucker took the easy way out. Slots and shots all night long, I'd sleep till noon and lunch by the pool, downing margaritas while I watched the girls in bikinis from behind the lenses of my designer shades.

Trevor Dent, on the other hand, never set foot in Sin City. When the old me died, I quit this place cold turkey. As I pilot the old truck down the Strip toward the Spire, my eyes pulled in every direction, I feel a bit seasick, overwhelmed by the gaudy decadence that used to whet my appetite. Still, I can't look away.

The Luxor . . . the Excalibur . . . New York, New York. All familiar to me, since I'd made the drunken walk back to the Spire more times than I can count. The last time, a few months before the cops put Gerry and my dad in cuffs and hauled them down to the station. A few months before Sidney disappeared. A few months before my father's secretary found him pale-faced and clutching his chest on the floor of his home office. A lot can happen in a few months.

Light-headed, I roll down my window, taking in a gulp of exhaust. Two Feather Girls in bright-pink bustiers and white go-go boots pose for pictures on the corner near the Cosmopolitan. One wiggles her fingers at me, smiling.

I slam the brakes, look again. The wind lifts her hair from across her face, and my heart sinks. It's not Paige after all. Of course it's not. Paige is somewhere dark and cold with duct tape around her wrists and mouth, her throat gone raw from screaming.

Anxious to be off this garish ride, I mash the accelerator, keeping my focus straight ahead until I make the U-turn by Fashion Valley. I zip back down the Strip, slowing when I spot the famous Bellagio fountains and the tourists gathered out front, crowding the sidewalk like pigeons. I turn in, passing the valet stand, opting to park it myself in the Spire garage, circling up to the fourth story.

After I hoist the go-bag over my shoulder, I don't look back. I pretend I belong here. Like Tanya will be happy to see me. It's as good a place as any to start the search for my dad's secret files.

When the elevator doors part, revealing the opulent hotel lobby, for a split second I forget who I am now. For a split second, it feels like home.

"Tanya Drucker's room, please."

The suit at the front desk nods coolly before passing me the receiver. "One moment, sir."

He directs his attention to the disgruntled guest behind me as I wait for Tanya's honeyed hello, every shrill ring sending a jolt down my spine. When she finally answers, I feel twenty-one again, standing in the Little White Chapel next to my father as he said *I do* to wife number four, otherwise known as Tanya May Givens. A twenty-nine-year-old showgirl who bore a striking resemblance to the wives before her.

"I have a delivery for Miss Drucker. Could I come up?"

"A delivery?" I hope I haven't miscalculated. I'd only known Tanya for a few months before my father made her a widow and the beneficiary of a perpetual comp; the high-roller suite he negotiated by gambling exclusively at the Spire and successfully representing its multimillionaire owner on charges of securities fraud. "From Louis Vuitton, I hope."

She doesn't let me down.

"That's the one," I say.

"The Chairman's Suite. Don't keep me waiting."

I hang up the phone myself—grateful that the suit didn't hear my white lie—and book it to the elevator, carrying my go-bag, a duffel purchased for ten bucks at an Austin Wal-Mart seven years ago. No Vuitton in sight.

Across the extravagant lobby, past the casino and the luxury boutiques, I know the way to the guest elevators by heart. The doors part, revealing my face in the mirrored wall. I stare for a moment. Not at the new Trevor Dent, but at the man lingering in the corridor behind me. He wears a familiar black suit and tie, a familiar predatory gaze. A shiny something on his lapel catches the light.

Our eyes lock, but he makes no move forward or back. When the other guests file in, obscuring his view, I fade into the corner, wondering if they can hear my heart thudding in my chest. Buttons are pressed . . . polite chatter ensues.

As the elevator closes, I force myself to look. The man is still standing there, waiting. A horrifying thought grips me. What goes up must come down.

The monstrous Chairman's Suite consumes the corner of the thirty-fifth floor. I hurry down the long hallway toward it, my head on a swivel, as if the goon from the lobby is on my tail. It's been seven years since I laid eyes on Tanya, but I press the bell hard three times, summoning her straightaway.

When the door finally opens a crack, Tanya barely notices me. But I can't look away from her meaty hand gripping the frame. Each doughy finger choked by the gold band of a cocktail ring. Minus the tasteless jewelry, these are not the hands of the Tanya I knew.

"Do I need to sign something?" Her voice is familiar, though. A thin veneer of civility disguises her impatience.

I clear my throat, drawing her attention to my face. She yelps, jumps back, and I won't deny I feel satisfied. My father had left the bulk of his estate to her, a woman he'd known for barely one year. One thing about Alan Drucker, he really knew how to stick it to you.

"Jesus Christ, you look a little like someone I used to know." She composes herself and opens the door a bit wider, revealing the rest of her. Same cotton-candy-pink lipstick. Same bottled blonde. Her dancer's body replaced by soft curves and a squishy midsection. "So where's my Vuitton?"

"Sorry." I shrug, dropping the go-bag between us. It lands with a thump. "It's been a long time. I wasn't sure you'd recognize me."

She squints at me, disbelieving. "Teddy?"

I nod briskly, alarmed by the elevator's sudden ding. Someone is coming. "Can we talk inside?"

"Uh—" Before she can refuse, I push my way in, dragging my bag behind me. She owes me this much.

Tanya paces the plush carpet from one end of the suite to the other, before she leans against the back of the sofa, a fifty-inch plasma playing *Real Housewives* on the wall behind her.

"I thought you were dead," she confesses, finally. "Or living in a hut on the beach in Mexico. The LAPD harassed me for a whole year, you know. They thought you were hiding out here."

If she's expecting an apology, she's out of luck.

"They said you had something to do with that girl's disappearance. Cindy, was it?"

Now she's just being cruel. But at least the news about Paige hasn't reached Vegas yet.

"Sidney Archer. And I didn't."

"That's what I told them. That you didn't have it in you."

Tanya manages to make it sound like a bad thing. But I leave it alone because she's given me more credit than I deserve. She has no idea what I'm capable of. I peer down the hallway toward the bedroom she once shared with my father.

"So what are you doing here?" she asks. "I won't loan you a penny if that's what you're after. Alan always said your mother spoiled you rotten." Her voice drops an octave, in her best impression of my dad. "Teddy hasn't had to work hard for anything a day in his life. A little adversity would do that boy some good."

"I don't want your money. But I do need your help."

She glances at the watch on her wrist. The bezel—diamond-encrusted, of course—glints in the sunlight that streams in through the floor-to-ceiling windows, casting rainbows on the ceiling. "It'll have to be quick. I have a facial booked for three thirty, and I prefer to take a steam beforehand. It opens the pores. Keeps me young and glowing."

I bite my tongue. I'm a psychologist now. A professional. I deal with difficult people for a living. Besides, as much as I'd like to tell her where to stick her pores, it won't get me any closer to what I need.

"Did my father ever mention the Lolita files?"

"Lolita files? You know your father and I never talked business. I wanted him to have fun. To enjoy life. That's why he loved me."

"Are you sure, Tanya? It's important."

I've already lost her. Her eyes drift to the door as she rubs the large stone on her ring finger.

"Did you keep any of his things? Maybe I could take a look?"

"Why now? You disappear like Jimmy Hoffa. Show up seven years later, here of all places, asking about Alan's files. It's suspicious if you ask me. Maybe I oughta let LAPD know you're sniffing around."

I sigh. I should've known how this would go. I'd blown my chances the moment I'd marched up to Tanya at my father's funeral, looked her right in the eyes, and called her a money-grubbing skank who'd used her powers of seduction to convince my father to change his will. Say what you want about Teddy Drucker, but he had some nerve. After all, my dad had left me enough money for the essentials. A Mini Cooper, a go-bag full of cash, a graduate degree. And an escort, of course.

"Listen, Tanya. I know I was out of line back then. No excuses. But I'm not that guy anymore. If you have those files, you might be in danger."

"You sound just like Gerry."

"Gerry? You mean Blackstone?" I try to contain my shock, but it leaks out anyway, staining my voice with bitterness, with suspicion. "You talked to him?"

Oblivious, Tanya rises from her roost. She's getting ready to give me the old heave-ho. "A few times. He called from San Quentin to check on me. We both struggled those first couple of years without your father. It was a comfort to hear a familiar voice. For him too, being wrongfully convicted like that. It must've taken a toll."

I study Tanya's face, uncertain. But the tears welling in her eyes confirm my worst fears. She really is that naïve.

"What did he tell you about the files?"

She waves me off with a flip of her hand and makes her way to the door. "Nothing really. He never mentioned anything specific. Only that Alan might've been privy to some sensitive information. By that time, I'd already packed up your father's office. Shredded the files, erased the laptop. Just like I was instructed in your father's will."

That's her final stone to throw, but it doesn't hit me as hard as she'd hoped. I'm too busy imagining the Lolita files buried unceremoniously in a landfill, stuck between a dirty diaper and an empty pizza box. Never to be seen again.

"Now, if you'll excuse me, I need to get to my facial. I remember you didn't much care about punctuality but . . ."

Tanya keeps talking. I don't hear a word. I'm laser-focused on the sliver of tan skin that's visible at the collar of her leisure wear. As she attempts to usher me toward the door, she catches me looking.

"That necklace," I say quickly, before she gets the wrong idea.

Her hand goes straight to it, covering it for a moment, then drops to her side again, revealing the antique chain, the gemmed pendant. "Isn't it striking?"

I nod, leaning in to examine it. Its familiarity, undeniable. "Where did you get it?"

"It was the last gift your father ever gave me."

CHAPTER 14

With the go-bag on my shoulder, I ease out of the Chairman's Suite, hopeful the suited man from the lobby isn't lurking outside the door, waiting to put a bullet in my head. That he's not one of Poseidon Security's goons. Nothing more than a figment of my paranoia.

Set on edge by the pin-drop quiet, I make my way down the empty hallway, searching for my own place to hide. I need to get back into Tanya's room, come hell or high water. She knows something. She must. Even if she's too air-headed to realize it. Besides, as much as it pains me, she's my only hope.

I duck down the stairwell as Tanya emerges from the suite and walks in the direction of the elevators. I listen for the open and shut of the mechanical door, poking my head out to confirm Tanya's absence. Then I book it straight for the house phone and dial 0.

"Spire Front Desk, how many I assist you?"

Be smooth, Trevor. "We're stepping out of the room for a bit. Would you send up housekeeping?"

"Certainly, sir. What room is that?"

"The Chairman's Suite."

"Right away, sir."

Satisfied with my performance, I pump my fist and let out a breath. Damn, I needed that.

But then, I hear it. The abrupt static of a walkie-talkie growing louder from the far hallway. I strain to make out the words.

"Possible sighting . . . suspect . . ."

As the hotel security guard rounds the corner, I slip out of sight, back into the confines of the stairwell. Fear rushes in, flooding my senses. Suddenly, it's too warm, too airless. My legs too heavy to move as fast as they should on the concrete steps. Especially with the go-bag weighing me down.

Above me, the door creaks open, and I freeze. Press myself to the wall like a lizard, wishing I could turn the same dreary gray. I imagine the guard there on the landing, his ears pricked like mine. Listening and waiting for me to reveal myself.

A bead of sweat trickles down my back. Lungs squeeze shut. Feet go numb. I'm not sure I can bear it any longer.

"No sign of anything. Returning to home base."

The door closes, but I don't move. Not yet. I can't risk it.

I watch the hands of my Rolex turn for a solid fifteen minutes before I inch out from the wall and peer upward into the empty stairwell. I drop to one knee and remove the Glock from my bag, tucking it into my waistband. I can't be too careful. Moving like a rabbit in the grass, I scamper up the steps and slip back into the hallway on high alert.

The maid cart sits at the far end of the hallway, parked outside the suite adjacent to Tanya's. A wooden sign hangs from the handle—YOUR ROOM IS BEING SERVICED. The dull roar of the vacuum inside.

I scan the hallway again before I sift through the toiletries, the sheets, the towels, the bathmats. The little chocolates with the Spire logo on a gold wrapper. I come up empty. No master key. Only a clipboard with the room numbers and the guests' statuses. Tanya's suite is marked *long-term resident.* After seven years leeching off the Drucker estate, I suppose that's one way to put it.

Frustrated, I double back to Tanya's front door, smacking it with my hand as I pass. To my surprise, it swings open, and

I lunge to catch it before it closes. I poke my head around the doorframe, listening. Satisfied with the silence, I skulk inside, marveling at Tanya's carelessness and my good fortune.

A fresh arrangement of pink lilies catches my eye from the vase on the console, which had been bare when Tanya tossed me out. Atop its rich mahogany surface rests a small greeting card, dated today.

Mrs. Drucker,

Please accept our sincerest apologies for the cancellation of your Spire spa service due to unexpected building maintenance. Present this card when rebooking your complimentary sixty-minute facial or massage. We look forward to your visit.

Sincerely,
The Spire Relaxation Team

Canceled? I take a single step forward, craning my neck to see around the corner. If Tanya catches me snooping around, the jig is up. She'd sell me out to Gerry or the cops or both in the time it takes to say sycophant.

I gently place the go-bag on the carpet and creep toward the half-open bedroom door at the end of the hallway.

The closer I get, the louder my heart drums in my chest, urging me to turn around. To go back the way I came before I end up flatlining just like my father. Dead on arrival. This is my chance, though, and I won't get another.

Cardiac arrest be damned, I press on, nudging the door the rest of the way with my foot.

A swath of sunlight streams in from the floor-to-ceiling window, cutting across the king-sized bed and onto the carpet. There, in the soft glow, Tanya's purse lays on its side, open. Its contents partly spilled.

The drawers of the dresser and the nightstand gape obscenely. Tanya's jewelry is scattered. Her undergarments, tossed about.

The mattress lays at a strange angle, as if it's been upended. The comforter, the throw pillows, even Tanya's pink slippers, are askew.

My mouth goes dry.

I take a step forward, then jump back, realizing I've crunched the Spire master key beneath my boot. I reach out to steady myself, staring in horror at my prints on the chrome-finished dresser.

This is a crime scene. I know that now.

A hand extends on the floor alongside the bed, limp. A cocktail ring on every fat finger.

CHAPTER 15

SEVEN YEARS EARLIER
TEDDY

Teddy couldn't sleep with Sidney curled against him. Even with the window open, her skin felt too hot against his. At least he'd managed to talk her off the ledge over chocolate scones.

Fast forward to her place and a few glasses of wine later, he'd finally gotten lucky. So really, a win-win. No matter what he'd promised her, Teddy had no intention of mentioning Sidney's complaints to his father. Because Alan Drucker would undoubtedly find some way to lay the blame at his feet. Blackstone wanted a Sidney-shaped unicorn. As much as it irked Teddy, the old guy pining after his girlfriend, what choice did he have?

As Teddy slipped from beneath the sheets, Sidney stirred. He waited for the sound of her breathing to slow before he tried again, freeing himself. He tugged on his boxer briefs and slunk toward her cell phone charging on the dresser.

She'd entrusted him with her password a few months ago. *In case of emergency*, she'd told him. But Teddy recognized it for what it was. A test of mutual trust. Which he'd failed, of course. No way in hell he'd grant her a free pass to his contact list. Especially now that he'd earned himself Most Eligible Bachelor honors. He planned to milk that little title through the summer at least. Even if it had been earned through Daddy's connections.

Glancing back to the bed, Teddy unlocked the cell and tapped the photos icon. When Sidney had shown him the photos she'd taken of the Erinnyes financials, he'd been dumbfounded. Teddy had no clue what Blackstone was up to. But he knew for certain his father wouldn't want Sidney sticking her delicate nose anywhere near it. And collecting photographic evidence? Hell, she should know better.

He deleted the first photo.

"Teddy?"

His heart throbbed as he stood there, frozen. Like he could blend into the wallpaper if he only stayed still enough.

"What are you doing?"

He heard Sidney rustling behind him. Imagined her searching for the silk La Perla robe he'd bought her for her birthday last month. Sheer and lacy, it was the kind of gift that kept on giving.

"Looking for my phone."

He felt her warmth behind him, though she hadn't touched him yet. "Are you going somewhere?"

He swallowed his guilt like a shard of bone, realizing she hadn't noticed her cell in his hand. All she saw was him leaving.

"Early morning training session with Bruce."

"I can set the alarm." Dejection dampened her voice. "As early as you'd like."

"It's at Runyon Canyon. That's ten minutes from my place. If I stay here, I'll get stuck in traffic. And you know what happens if I'm late." Gently placing the phone onto the dresser, he turned toward her and took her face in his hands. Kissed her with his lying mouth. "Twenty extra ab hits with the med ball."

"I'm worth it though, right?"

He tugged at the tie on her robe. Marveling for a moment at her perfect breasts, he slipped his arms inside the cool fabric and around her naked body. As he backed them both toward the bed, he peeked over his shoulder. The phone still glowed, bright as a neon sign behind him. It went unnoticed.

CHAPTER 16

WEDNESDAY LATE AFTERNOON
4 P.M.
LAS VEGAS, NEVADA

Tanya's head droops awkwardly to one side of her arm, revealing the purplish groove that circles her neck; the mark the same width as the thick cord that powers the hairdryer that has been tossed on the bed.

Her pale face gazes downward at the carpet, unseeing. Her eyes, bulging and blood-red.

Sickened, I watch for signs of life. But her chest remains as still as my shadow.

I need to run. To get the hell out of here. But it's only my mind that races, trying to make sense of the unthinkable.

Tanya, dead. Strangled. Her bedroom, rifled through. Yet, the obnoxious diamond ring my father gave her eight years ago remains on her finger, twinkling in the sunlight. The others too. And a glance into the open drawer—still strewn with gold bangles and emerald hoop earrings and a tangle of gemmed necklaces—tells me this was no random robbery. The killer had something specific in mind. Or the plan to make it appear that way.

It hits me then like a shot of cold water, and I rush back to Tanya's body to be sure. Her mangled neck is bare.

I drop to my knees, tilting my head to search the shadows alongside her slumping body. The cave of darkness beneath the bed. Nothing.

I scramble to my feet. Tucking my hand inside the hem of my shirt—a makeshift glove—I paw through the tangle of jewelry until I reach the drawer's smooth wooden bottom.

The noise comes from behind me, and I spin toward it, stifling a yelp. The room remains empty. I reach for my gun, grateful for its weight in my trembling hand, and point it at center mass. The oak slats of the coat closet.

I take a step forward, psyching myself up. Do it already. Squeeze the trigger.

I picture the old me, showing off for my frat buddies, draining my dad's Desert Eagle 50 while they whooped and whistled. But this isn't the Elite Gun Club. And that's no paper target.

One more step and I swallow hard. It's now or never.

"I hear you in there. Come out or I'll shoot." My voice sounds strangely breathy, but it cuts right through the whoosh of terror in my brain. Steadying my aim, I take an audible breath. Not trusting my eyes, I squint at the brass knob as it slowly turns.

The door creaks open.

"It's me." Lina crouches beneath the rack of clothing, pushing aside the long mink coat that drapes by her face.

"What are you doing here? How did you—" I stop talking and follow her eyes to the Glock, still extended in my hand. "I could've shot you."

As Lina crawls from the closet, I glance back to Tanya's lifeless body. A chill works its way up my spine. "Maybe I should have."

"I didn't kill her if that's what you're getting at."

"Well, who did?"

"Who do you think?" Lina struggles to her feet, her fist balled tightly at her side.

"What's in your hand?" I gesture with the gun's barrel, wielding it with a sudden rush of power.

"We've got to get out of here, Trevor. In case you didn't notice, your father's widow is on the floor. And she's very, very dead."

I wave the gun at Lina, my confusion spreading like a virus. How does she know Tanya? How did she get here?

"Open your hand. *Now.*"

"Or what? Are you really gonna shoot me?" She walks toward me, unafraid, her arms open wide. "Because that would be stupid. The place would be crawling with cops. But fine, be my guest. Put a bullet in my head."

Drunk with anger at the nerve of her, I fling the gun onto the bed and grab her by the arm, wrestling it behind her back. She struggles, but I only tighten my grip. Her arm feels as fragile as a bird's wing beneath my fingers. Breakable, like Sidney's.

That thought makes me pull back fast. As if her skin is on fire.

Spotting an opening, Lina nails me with an elbow to the jaw that rattles my teeth. I rub the sore spot, breathing hard, as we both stare at the carpet. At the necklace she dropped from her hand.

I get there first, scooping it up and into my palm. "Is this Tanya's?"

She half shrugs, half nods, which I take as a yes. I try not to look at the red mark on her arm. Because I did that, and I can't let myself feel bad for her. Not now.

"And the other one? The one you stole from me?" I tuck the delicate chain into my pocket.

"It's in the glove box of the Impala."

"The Impala? As in the green rust bucket we found in El Paso?"

"*I* found. And I paid cash."

"Yeah. *My* cash."

Lina rolls her eyes. "What did you expect, leaving me like that? I thought we had an understanding."

"Understanding, huh? You haven't been straight with me from the beginning."

"Like you have?"

The front door snaps shut, and we both go silent. In a haze of panicked desperation, I point to the closet, securing the gun before I follow Lina inside and pull the door shut, entombing us in the airless dark.

There's no time to hide ourselves. We push against the clothing and press into each other. Keeping a finger to my lips, I hold my breath and wait, the Glock still ready at my side.

"Housekeeping." The voice belongs to a woman. "Hello? Mrs. Drucker?"

She calls out again, her voice louder. I peer through the slats as the housekeeper enters the bedroom. The woman freezes. Looks for a long, long time at Tanya's body.

Then her hands begin to shake.

She hides her mouth behind her fingers, but nothing can muffle the sound of her scream.

I burst out of the closet into the unnerving quiet. We don't have much time. Not since the housekeeper hightailed it out of here in a frenzy.

Lina follows me out of the bedroom, staying close behind. No choice but to stick together now. We don't speak, and we don't look back. Every step toward the front door wrenches my stomach, but there's no stopping now. I listen hard, then ease the door open, pointing Lina to the stairwell down the hall.

We hustle down the first few flights before Lina stops cold, her face contorted in despair.

"There are cameras on every floor. They'll think I did it. That I killed Tanya."

I churn the blade of my hand through the air to try to keep her moving. But she's stock-still and stopped in the middle of the steps.

"What about me? They already think I killed Paige. Besides, if the cameras saw us, they saw the bad guys too. The cops aren't stupid."

"Those bad guys you're talking about . . . Poseidon? They're high tech. No chance of their faces showing up on the tape. If we get arrested now, they win. No one will ever see those files. It's up to us, Trevor. We have the key."

As we race down to the casino floor, her words sink in, dragging me down like quicksand.

Lina pushes through the exit and into the madness of the casino. The bright lights, the raucous shouting, the celebratory ring of a winning pull. She strides forward, and I follow, until we're both swallowed by the crowd.

"Wait," I call after her, struggling to keep up. But she doesn't slow down as she navigates her way through the maze of tables and slot machines. I try to make sense of what she said, but I have to stay focused on her chestnut hair, her denim jacket. I'm two, three, four steps behind, playing catch-up in more ways than one.

When Lina reaches the front lobby of the Spire, she freezes. She looks over her shoulder, her eyes landing on mine, before she whips her head back to the sprawling marble floors decorated for the upcoming Chinese New Year. I follow her tense gaze to the hotel entrance—to a group of men with stiff black suits and matching earpieces.

Lina backtracks toward me. "Check out their lapels," she says as she brushes past, taking up a position behind an ornate pillar.

Spotting their trident pins, I curse under my breath. "All of them?"

The Poseidon team assembles on the concourse outside the Spire, flanking a man I vaguely recognize. Tall and distinguished, he reminds me of Blackstone himself, the way he floats, unencumbered, from his motorcade into the lobby. The heavy doors open for him, the crowd parts. He brushes a hand through his salt-and-pepper hair and flashes a smile at the young woman behind the front desk.

Lina takes another quick look, her face paling as the man glides toward us with the Poseidon thugs in tow. They walk, nearly in unison, their jackets swishing open to reveal the sidearms at their hips.

By the time I find the butt of my gun, the group has passed us. They turn right, approach one of the large hotel ballrooms, and usher the man inside. A large banner billows above the threshold.

RE-ELECT DAVID CRAWLEY
U.S. SENATOR

I find myself knee-deep in a memory, seated with my father at Smith and Wollensky on our last business trip to Vegas. A hunk of bone-in rib eye in my mouth, a man had approached the table. David Crawley had introduced himself, shaken my hand, and then whisked my father off to a dark corner to talk.

"Poseidon works for Senator Crawley?"

Lina nods as we book it for the front doors. Outside, I suck in a breath of cold air, giddy with relief. But Lina looks as frightened as I've ever seen her.

"Do you know him?" My ears prick at the wail of a siren in the distance. So much for my momentary reprieve.

The shrieking grows louder until it drowns out all other sounds. Until we have no choice but to run.

Lina matches me stride for stride while her voice rings out, clear and startling as a gunshot. "Crawley was one of Gerry's regulars. He's on the snuff film."

There's no better place to disappear than the Las Vegas Strip after dark. As the sun dips below the Spring Mountains, Lina and I lay low in the crowd of tourists milling in front of the Bellagio Fountains, biding time—the one thing we don't have. From here, we can see the mounting troop of police cars blocking the Spire's front entrance, parking garage included. No one allowed in or out.

With a furtive crouch, I deposit the Glock inside the go-bag while Lina casually props her elbows on the concrete railing, like any other girl anticipating the magic of the dancing fountains. But I see it all in her eyes. The fear, the fatigue, the desperation. It's dulled the blue of her irises to gray, the color of a stormy sea.

"Why didn't you tell me that Poseidon worked for Crawley?" I speak the first in a long line of questions sprouting like weeds, demanding to be plucked. Asking questions. This is how a therapist copes.

"I didn't know for sure. Not until now." The music starts. The crowd gasps as the first burst of water shoots into the twilight. "It makes sense though. With a wife and two kids and White House ambitions, he has a lot to lose."

"Who else is on that tape?"

Lina purses her lips, side-eyeing me. "Oh, so *now* you believe me?"

"I'm not sure what to believe. But Tanya's dead for a reason. She must've known about the files. Maybe about Crawley too."

The fountains twirl higher and higher amid the bright lights, Lina's laughter lost in the applause. "Have you met Tanya? She had no clue what your dad had gotten himself into with Blackstone. She didn't want to know."

Lina isn't wrong. Even after my father got arrested, Tanya stuck by his side, perky as ever, bound by a healthy dose of greed and naivete.

"You knew Tanya?"

"Not really. But I knew of her. Gerry called her your dad's trailer-trash trophy."

My grimace is more guilt than anything, because it sounds like the kind of thing I would've said, drunk on spite. Lina's staring out at the cascading water, apparently too lost in her memories to notice.

"When you said you wanted to stop in Vegas, I figured you were headed to the Spire to see her. I swiped the master key from housekeeping to poke around a little. When Tanya came back, I hid in the closet and waited. Then the Poseidon thugs showed up. They pushed their way in and started ransacking the place, looking for something. Tanya fought back, and—"

The fountains firework as the music reaches a crescendo. Lina jumps back, slightly startled. I play out the rest of the scene, the way it must've gone. Tanya strangled with the hairdryer cord while Lina watched through the slats, trying not to breathe.

"Did they say anything to her about what they were looking for?"

As the crowd applauds and begins to disperse, Lina pushes back from the railing and studies me. Like she's trying to work out if I'm really *that* stupid. "The key, obviously. To your dad's safe."

"The key?"

Lina shoves her hand into her pocket, removing a necklace that looks suspiciously similar to my father's, to the one she stole from me.

"I thought you said you left it in the glove box."

The corner of her mouth hints at a smile. "This beauty is way too valuable to leave in a glove box."

I hold out my hand, waiting, but she doesn't return it as I expect. Instead, she pinches the top of the small pendant just above the row of gemstones and pulls, revealing a serrated edge.

"What the hell are you doing?"

"I need the other one. Tanya's."

Hurriedly, I dig in my pocket for the matching necklace. Securing the pendant between my thumb and forefinger, I hold it up, easily spotting the thin break in the metal. This pendant, just like its match, is cut into two pieces. I tug at the end, the way Lina did. The top snaps off, and I'm left to stare, open-mouthed, at its innards.

"This is the key?"

I hadn't given my father enough credit. Lina either, for that matter. If Alan Drucker had gone to these lengths to protect his files, the contents must be A-bomb level.

"Part of it," Lina says, fitting it against the other piece. Like a magnet, the teeth snap together. She drops it carefully into the front flap of her blue jean jacket. "There's a third section. We have to find it."

"And then what?"

Lina blinks at me, wide-eyed, her gaze fixed behind me. I prepare myself for impact. For a bullet to the back from a man wearing a trident pin.

Instead, a voice stops me cold.

"Police. Hands up, both of you."

I contemplate making a break for it, losing myself in the dispersing crowd. But Lina has the necklace, and I'm exactly nowhere without it.

The officer shoves me forward into the concrete railing, and I fold over in surrender, wincing at the ache in my ribs. After he's secured my hands, he spins me around by the elbow, so that we're eye to eye. His name tag reads MOREHEAD.

"That bag belong to you?" It's one of *those* questions again. He already knows the answer. The bag sits on the sidewalk between me and Lina, undeniably ours.

Before Lina can talk us into more trouble, I clear my throat with purpose, give her a little head shake, and she stays silent. An officer swoops in, seizing the bag, while another leads Lina away from me.

"Do you know Tanya Drucker?" Morehead thinks he's on a roll now.

But twenty-two years of living in Alan Drucker's legalistic shadow is finally good for something. My words belong to him. "I invoke my right to remain silent."

CHAPTER 17

SEVEN YEARS EARLIER
SIDNEY

As soon as Teddy stumbled out the door at 5 a.m. for his weekly ass-kicking with Bruce, Sidney dashed to the bathroom. She splashed her face, brushed her teeth, and slicked her hair back into a sleek ponytail. Thirty minutes later, she arrived at Calypso headquarters and headed for the small file cabinet behind Marsha's chair. Just yesterday, Marsha had retrieved the site plans from inside it, unlocking it with the silver key she kept in the center drawer of her desk.

Sidney tugged at the drawer a few times, hard. It didn't give. But she'd come prepared. Slipping her nail file from the pocket of her slacks, she knelt in front of the desk and shimmied the tool into the space above the lip of the drawer. When she heard a soft click, she nearly yelped with excitement.

With the key in hand, she unlocked the file cabinet and scanned its contents, careful to only touch what she needed. To leave it the way she'd found it. She snapped a photo, locked the drawer, and retreated to her office, giddy.

Hunkering at her desk, she enlarged the photograph of the registration document for Erinnyes Corporation. The business had been registered in 2005 to Michael Bodden of Grand Cayman. A quick internet search revealed Erinnyes's sleek website that promised its clients access to the most-exclusive properties in the Cayman Islands. Bodden himself had a flashy Facebook page. In his profile picture, he posed alongside an exotic car, a voluptuous young woman draped across the hood.

After calculating the two-hour time difference, Sidney dialed the number on the website and waited, listening to the sound of her breath.

"Erinnyes Realty. How can I help you?"

"Is this Michael Bodden?"

"The one and only. What can I do for you?"

Sidney's stomach twisted. She hadn't really thought this through. "My husband and I would like to purchase some property on Grand Cayman. Something near the beach. Do you have any listings you could show us? Something in the one-million-dollar range."

"No properties for sale at the moment, but I'd be happy to take your number and get back to you."

Instead, Sidney fired off a few more questions. "What was the last property you sold? Is there someone I could speak to for a reference? We want to be sure we're working with an agent we can trust."

"Oh sure. Give me a moment." Sidney listened to the shuffling of papers. "You can call Erik Gordon. He just closed on a beautiful beachfront home in Crystal Harbor. A spacious four bedroom—"

Sidney returned the phone to its cradle trying not to panic. She'd never met Blackstone's body man, Erik "Gordo" Gordon, but she'd heard the other paralegals whisper his name as if they'd been afraid of conjuring the devil himself. When she'd naively asked Marsha about him, Marsha had said simply, "Best you never know, dear."

****

At noon, Sidney's cell dinged, alerting her to a new text. Knowing Blackstone would return from New York that day, she'd been tiptoeing on eggshells all morning, listening for footfalls outside her door while searching futilely for more information on Erinnyes Corporation.

Now, she'd been summoned by the man himself.

Meet me at my hotel in an hour.

Sidney thought of quitting right then. She could start over at a new firm. Maybe even take a break for a while. Go home and visit her parents. Convince them not to be worried about her. That she *hadn't* changed since she'd moved to the city. That she was still the same small-town girl.

I have your holiday bonus.

Sidney frowned at the screen. Bonus? If she planned to give notice, she could certainly use it. Surely, she could handle Blackstone for one more day.

As she gathered her things, a long shadow darkened her door. She glanced up into the expectant face of Senator Crawley. "Ms. Archer, we meet again."

"Uh—hi." She tried to make sense of the politician standing in her office as if he belonged there. "I was just on my way out. Mr. Blackstone asked me to meet him."

"Did he? Well, Gerry can wait."

In Sidney's experience, he most certainly could not, but she simply nodded. "How can I help you?"

"Get a drink with me. Let's get to know each other better." He stepped in further, closing the door behind him. "Gerry told me you're interested in advancing your career, whatever it takes. He said you've been quite eager, quite amenable to suggestion."

Sidney heard her purse drop to the floor. Felt her mouth open slightly. The blood rushed to her face. Before she could react, Crawley had arranged himself in front of her, his long limbs blocking her exit.

"So, what do you say?"

"No."

One little word but it packed a wallop. Crawley reared back as if she'd slapped him.

"No?"

"No. I can't have a drink with you. I don't mean to be disrespectful, but that wouldn't be appropriate." Sidney reached for her bag and pushed past the senator. "I have a boyfriend."

"Teddy Drucker, you mean? I must have misunderstood. I didn't realize the two of you were exclusive. Gerry insinuated that he was one of many. That you like to mix business and pleasure. And so do I."

Ripping the door open, Sidney could finally breathe again. Beyond the threshold, curious heads poked above cubicles, eyes trained on her office. Her voice must have been louder than she'd thought.

"You were mistaken, Senator." She lowered her voice, hissed at him, "Now see yourself out before I make a scene."

Windows down, radio cranked, Sidney drove to the Beverly Wilshire, already feeling better. She left the car with the valet, expensing the charge to the Penthouse Suite, and hurried to the fourteenth floor, eager to put Blackstone and Calypso in her rearview. After her run-in with Crawley, her future finally felt decided. She wanted nothing more than to make the three-hour drive back to Kernville and spend the weekend, possibly the month, bingeing bad TV on her parents' couch and eating ice cream by the tablespoon.

Before she could raise her finger to press the bell, the door flung open. A brute of a man stood over her. His cue-ball head seemed too small for the rest of his body. He sized her up with the eyes of a reptile.

"Ms. Archer, I presume?"

"Sidney." She gulped. "I don't believe we've met."

"Gordo," he said, pointing to himself. He gestured for her to come inside, shutting the door behind her. The sound of it reverberated through her body, taking her back to her office with Crawley and raising goosebumps on her skin.

"Sit, Ms. Archer. *Sidney*."

She took the nearest chair, perching on the edge of it, her foot tapping out her apprehension in a frenzied Morse code.

"Mr. Blackstone asked me to speak with you on his behalf. To remind you of the importance of your discretion and loyalty. To him. To your employers, Drucker and Webber. And Calypso, by extension."

He laid a check on the glass coffee table. She gaped at it—twenty-five thousand dollars made out to her from Erinnyes Corporation—but didn't dare reach for it. She already knew it came with strings.

"Take it," Gordo said. "It's yours."

"And if I don't?"

"Then you really are a dumb blonde." Gordo's hacking laugh lasted as long as it took him to place a photograph on her lap. The image enlarged and printed on copy paper. Slightly blurry but recognizable. She held it between her fingers, watching it shake like a leaf in the wind.

"This sort of thing could destroy a woman. If it got out, that is. Climbing the corporate ladder on your back isn't a good way to start a career." It wasn't a question, but she felt her head bob up and down. "Good, you naughty girl. We understand each other then."

Sidney reached for the check to appease him, but he grabbed her by the wrist, stopping her short.

"A word of advice. Next time you want to stick your nose where it doesn't belong, don't use the office phone."

As soon as the elevator door shut behind her, Sidney collapsed to the cold floor. No wonder Crawley had the wrong idea about her. She forced herself to look again at the photograph, captured from outside the open window of her studio apartment early this morning. Her breasts bared, her legs spread, with Teddy Drucker standing between them.

CHAPTER 18

WEDNESDAY NIGHT
5 P.M.
LAS VEGAS, NEVADA

Lina glares at me from her side of the patrol car like it's my fault her hands are cuffed behind her back. She and her trusty stun gun in the custody of the Las Vegas Metropolitan PD.

We haven't been arrested yet, only detained, but the cold metal bites into my wrists, reminding me how guilty I am. How much I've done wrong. Getting rid of the Drucker name could never change that. Even with the good I've done as a therapist, I can't wipe the slate. Teddy is still in here, culpable as ever.

"Now what?" Lina hisses.

"We don't speak. Not to each other. Not to them. Got it?"

By *them*, I mean the cops shooting the shit outside the window, taking their sweet time while the minutes tick by, inching Paige closer to her eventual doom. Sticking me and Lina in here together, they must be waiting for us to blow it, counting on it even. Which means they don't have the evidence to prove a goddamn thing without our help. Yet.

But they've already opened the go-bag, holding up the Glock like the head of some exotic beast they felt lucky to snare. One of the officers unloaded it and locked it in his trunk. Once they trace it back to a dead guy, it'll be game over. They'll pin Tanya's murder on us too. On me, specifically. Since I'm the one who's left a wake of missing women behind me.

Lina says nothing more, and I refuse to look at her. It would only break my will. I focus on the small tear in the vinyl seat in front of me, pretending I'm back in my office on South Congress leading my own guided meditation. It's the only way to stop the platoon of panicked thoughts that's been parading through my head since the cops shoved me back here and dumped my duffel in an evidence bag in the trunk. Marching front and center, the realization that soon Teddy Drucker will be unmasked, a spotlight shone on the past life I kept carefully hidden. All my secrets laid bare.

Finally, Officer Morehead flings open the front door and slides into the driver's seat with a grunt. "The detectives want a word downtown."

I grunt right back, taking a page from Detective Vega's partner. At least she hasn't shown up yet, Turkey in tow, to make me look worse than I already do.

Another officer directs pedestrian traffic as the cruiser eases onto the Strip. At the first red light, I risk a glance at Lina. Stupid mistake. She leans her head against the window, avoiding me. I hope she didn't tell the cops anything stupid. Like the truth.

We round the block and take a right onto busy Las Vegas Boulevard. The traffic only delays our inevitable arrival at the station, our meet-cute with another set of eagle-eyed detectives who will take whatever liberties they need to drive a wedge between us.

Every stop at a red light ratchets up my anxiety.

This is bad.

Really bad.

Beyond bad.

Morehead radios the station before he takes a left onto the less-traveled East Harmon Avenue. Snaking down a few more deserted side streets, the car picks up speed, careening me toward the metaphorical cliff's edge. The point of no return. Past when time runs out and Paige dies, and I'm left holding the bag.

The Pinball Hall of Fame appears in the side window. It seems appropriate for the last two days. For the way my heartbeat ricochets like a marble through my rib cage. But Morehead's steely eyes in the rearview remind me this is no game. No gumball prize awaits me. Only a mounting stack of evidence and a six-by-nine cell.

A flash of movement, and Lina tenses in my periphery. As I turn toward her, she sucks in a tight breath at the black pickup truck barreling down the alley like a wild bull, its front end aimed directly at the side of the patrol car.

Morehead curses and yanks the wheel to swerve while I brace for impact, gritting my teeth. Lina's cry gets lost in the screech of metal on metal, the explosion of the airbag, my frantic gasps.

The driver's side of the patrol car crumples, sending shards of glass raining down from the broken windshield. Lina catapults into me, both of us smashed against the window, tossed about in the storm.

My head smacks the glass, leaving me dizzy and spinning and seeing stars. The car spins too, round and round like a roulette wheel. Finally, it comes to rest pointing the wrong way. Visible through the cracks, another black sedan blocks traffic at the end of the street.

Lina slumps across my lap, moaning. From above her eye, a cut weeps onto the sweatshirt she chose for me.

Morehead makes no sound at all, and I'm grateful when my vision blurs to a gauzy haze, obscuring the forward droop of his head and the sheer whiteness of his exposed arm bone.

Clawing my way back to consciousness, I turn my eyes upward to the familiar man approaching the door. He flings it open and lugs me out by the arms, dropping me to the asphalt in disgust. I flump over in a heap, fading in and out.

"Get up." Gordo practically spits the words at me. "Now."

I want to tell him to go straight to hell. That I can't get up with my hands cuffed behind my back. But then I realize he's already freed me and the go-bag, which now rests at my feet. And he's not alone. The crashed truck sits empty, its driver—one of Gordo's henchman, no doubt—sneers at me. Like he'd just as soon put a bullet in my head. Put me out of my misery.

Instead, he stalks over to the patrol car and tries to wrestle open the mangled door with his gloved hands. Failing, he reaches through the hole that used to be the window, its frame broken out and contorted, and produces Morehead's service weapon. He returns to stand over me, dropping the gun on top of the go-bag.

I shake my head. "Hell, no. I don't want that thing."

"No one asked you," Gordo answers for him, unzipping the bag and placing the Glock inside it. "If anyone else gets those files, I have to answer to Gerry. And if I have to answer to Gerry, heads roll. Yours included. Got it?"

The distant sound of sirens spurs me to my feet. Thanks to Poseidon, the Strip is crawling with cops. Surely, they'll be here in no time.

"What about Lina?"

"What about her?" As Gordo leers at Lina, half awake in the back seat, his meaty paw massages his gun in his waistband.

"I need her with me. She knows how to find the files. I can't do it without her. I won't."

"Suit yourself." Gordo points toward the dark sedan idling nearby. "But if you ask me, you're better off without her. That girl can't be trusted." He carelessly tosses a key ring in my direction.

While Gordo's armed goon follows him into another vehicle, I scramble to catch the keys, watching forlornly as they clatter against the asphalt.

Two keys—car and handcuff—hang from the metal loop, attached to a plastic Las Vegas emblem that reads WHAT HAPPENS IN VEGAS . . . If only that were true. I have no doubt that what's happened here will be staggering after us like the undead. A horde of zombies in our rearview.

Keys in hand, I rush back to the patrol car, to Lina. She's managed to sit up, her feet planted firmly on the street, even if the rest of her looks a little woozy. Swaying to one side, she braces her hand against the seat.

"Is that—" Her eyes track over my shoulder. "Gordo?"

With a quick nod, I reach around Lina to insert the small pin in the handcuffs' lock. They spring open, and I haul her to her feet, half carrying her to the sedan's open door. Once she's secured in the back with the go-bag, I head for the driver's seat.

A photograph affixed to the wheel stops me cold. All my nightmares come to life. *Paige.* Her eyes red from crying, a thick strip of duct tape wrapped around the mouth I long to kiss. Her dark hair matted beneath it. I rip it off to find a message scrawled on the back.

Don't underestimate me the way your father did.

It's not signed, but I recognize the messy handwriting of Alan Drucker's best client. I stuff the photo in the pocket of my jeans, wishing I could burn it. Rub Blackstone's bloodied face in the ashes.

A honking horn spurs me to life, and I look up to find another sedan gliding past. Gordo rides shotgun with the passenger window rolled down and that same sleazeball smirk that reminds me of my father, that tells me he's holding a winning hand.

"Tick, tock, Teddy. Tick, tock."

****

I pilot the sedan to the freeway, checking the rearview on repeat and muttering under my breath like one of my patients.

"Four hours to LA. In the city by 10 p.m., 11 at the latest. Five hours to find the rest of the key, locate the files, and rescue Paige. No biggie." I laugh out loud, sounding slightly unhinged.

"Who are you talking to?" Lina asks from the back seat.

I jump, clenching the wheel even tighter. "I thought you were resting."

She sits up and leans forward, looking in the mirror and dabbing at her face. At least the cut has stopped bleeding, but the garish trail of dried blood clings stubbornly to her forehead and cheek.

"As soon as we get out of Nevada, we can stop at a gas station to clean up."

"I'm not sure that's a good idea." Lina crawls across the console and into the passenger seat.

She's probably right. The last thing we need is another close call.

"Are we just going to pretend that didn't happen back there?" she asks, buckling her safety belt.

"Fine by me."

But even as I say it, the entire cursed day plays back like a bad movie. From leaving Lina behind to finding her again. To Tanya, strangled. And finally, to Gordo doing what Gordo does best. Whatever it takes to keep Blackstone satisfied. I imagine him lurking behind us, following our taillights in the dark.

"Did that cop—was he . . .?"

"Probably. Three thousand pounds of steel aimed right at him. What do you expect?"

Lina doesn't answer, just stares out the window, and I feel like a prick. An honest prick but a prick all the same.

"Sorry. I didn't mean to sound so harsh. It's like I'm in a dream. Secret files, a hidden key. Bodies piling up around us. None of this feels real."

"Do you think Gordo knows we have these?" She reaches into her front pocket and removes the pendants, fitting them together again in the overhead light.

"Gordo knows everything."

Lina shakes her head at me. "Surely if he knew about these, he would've killed us both and taken them for himself."

"But then, he'd never find the last piece of the puzzle. He needs us."

A slight raise of her eyebrows makes me wonder how much Lina heard back there. If she realizes she's expendable.

"So how did you know about the pendants?"

"I watched your father open the safe once." She speaks so softly I strain to hear her over the hum of the asphalt under our wheels.

"You saw him?"

Silently, she coils the necklaces, transferring them from one palm to the other until she finally returns them to her front pocket. "Your father planned to testify against Gerry. He had the means—the ledger of Gerry's dirty secrets—and the motive. The DA had offered him a sweet deal."

I can barely keep my focus on the road. It doesn't help that it's pitch-black out here. That the scorched earth on either side resembles the surface of a distant planet. "How do you know so much about my dad?"

Lina sighs, as if the answer should be obvious. As if speaking it aloud might hurt. I brace for impact.

"It was Gerry's idea. He wanted me to get close to your father, to seduce him on video. An insurance policy, that's what Gerry called it. He had one on everybody. It's why he kept me around for so long. I was good at getting powerful men to make very big mistakes."

The familiar worm of disgust writhes in my stomach, same as it did the day that I'd forked over the bail money and driven my father home, both of us pretending the words *unlawful sex with a minor* didn't apply to him.

"You were the one he had sex with? You're Victim Three?"

The slightest nod of Lina's head breaks me.

"God, Lina. I had no idea. I'm sorry." So small a word. Necessary but insufficient. "Why did you see him again? Didn't the judge issue a no-contact order?"

"They asked me to see him. The cops hoped I could convince him to help with the case against Gerry, and he agreed. On New Year's Day, he told me to meet him at his house. He showed me Gerry's ledger and the laptop with all the photos and videos. He was shaken up, afraid. He'd changed his mind about cooperating. But he wanted me to know where the evidence was in case something happened to him. I think he felt guilty. Like he owed me. Which he damn well did."

"Why did he change his mind? Why didn't he tell me? Why didn't he tell me *any* of this?" My voice betrays me. I'm still eight years old and running after my father like he hung the moon. No matter what he's done, what he did, I could never stop wanting him to notice me. That kind of hopeful foolishness comes hard-wired. "I'm his only goddamn kid."

"I'm sure he would've told you if he could. He thought he was in danger. That he'd seen too much. That's why he ended up dead." Gently, Lina adds, "When you see the files for yourself, you'll understand. He probably wanted to protect you."

"My father had a heart attack. The coroner said so."

Lina touches my arm resting on the console, and I flinch. From her touch. From her words too. The shock of them burns through me like a lightning strike.

"Oh, Trevor. You don't really believe he died of natural causes, do you?"

I don't tell Lina the truth. That I'd never given it a second thought. That I'd been too worried about saving my own ass to insist on an autopsy. That a part of me felt relieved to wriggle out from under Alan Drucker's massive shadow. I know she's right. The note on the back of that horrific photo all but confirmed it.

"He had heart disease. Acute myocardial infarction. That's how he died."

Lina pulls her hand back, lays it in her lap, shrugs. "Believe what you want. But in my opinion, his betrayal killed him. You don't double-cross Gerry Blackstone and go on living."

"And yet here you are."

She cocks her head at me. "Here we *both* are."

"Only because we have something he wants."

"Well, not exactly," she says. "We only have part of it. It's useless without the third piece. We can't even be sure it's in LA."

"I'm sure." Though I'm not sure at all. It's only wishful thinking. "Hey, I'm sorry about leaving you in El Paso. It's just that—"

"It's okay," Lina interrupts me. "I heard what Gordo said to you about me. That I can't be trusted. That you're better off without me."

I wince, hoping she doesn't change her mind now that we've come this far. In front of us, the blacktop meets the inky sky, making it impossible to tell where one ends and the other begins.

"He wants to get rid of you."

"Don't kid yourself. He wants to get rid of both of us. But the only way we win here is to trust each other."

"You lied to me. You stole from me. You elbowed me in the face. From where I'm sitting, Gordo might be right."

"And you've done better?"

Score one for Lina.

"But you still trust me?" I ask, cataloguing all the reasons why she shouldn't.

In the dark cave of the car, I can't read her face, but I imagine the hint of a smile. "As much as I could ever trust the son of Alan Drucker."

****

Somewhere in the middle of the Mojave Desert, with LA still two hours away, Lina speaks the question aloud. The only one that matters now. The one I've come back to again and again, ever since she first fitted those two pendants into place. "So where is the third piece?"

I squint at the road ahead, my eyes gritty with fatigue. In the headlight's bright beam, I find only blacktop. It's been at least an hour since an armadillo scuttled in the weeds at the edge of my vision. The last living soul we'd seen. "I told you. It's in LA."

"But where exactly? LA's a big place, and we don't have much—"

I smack the wheel harder than I intend, sending a jolt of pain up my arm. "Don't you think I know that?"

A flash of Paige again. The way the duct tape snagged at her hair, twisted her delicate skin into a garish mask.

"Even if we find the third piece, there's no guarantee we can access the safe. My dad set up a trust to fund the estate. Covington House is a historical landmark now. A museum with guided tours and private security."

In the years after I disappeared, curiosity got the better of me. Sent me searching the internet for news of the house too big and too fancy to grow a boy up properly. Built in the 1920s by a famed architect, it had been purchased by a movie studio mogul who'd been known to host Gatsby-esque parties with guest lists that read like a who's who of Old Hollywood. Rumor had it Clark Gable had romanced Lana Turner on a bench in the gardens. After my dad had bit the dust, the city declared it an invaluable piece of Hollywood history. Every New Year's Eve, they held a Gatsby-themed party for their donors.

"We'll have to break in," Lina says. "Obviously."

"For all we know, the safe was already discovered years ago. It could be empty."

Lina scoffs at me like I'm a total amateur. "No way. If anybody found it, trust me, you'd know. The whole world would."

"So why didn't you go to the cops? They would've gotten a warrant, opened the safe, and put Blackstone away forever. And you and I wouldn't be here right now driving on a road to hell."

Lina swallows hard. Here I go again, saying the wrong thing. Victim blaming.

"Why do you think? I was fifteen and scared out of my mind. I'd already seen what Gerry could do. The kind of power he had. I didn't want to end up starring in a snuff film. Not to mention the money."

"The money?"

"After my mom died last year, I took a look through her bank statements. Calypso Development Group had paid her one hundred thousand dollars back then for some consulting work. Which made no sense. My mom didn't even finish high school. She could barely hold down a job as a maid. A few weeks after your father died, she picked us up and moved us cross-country to a brand-new apartment in Raleigh, North Carolina. She told me she'd won the money from a scratch-off ticket."

A pair of headlights approach in the distance, momentarily blinding me. I lower the high beams and pray to God it's not Poseidon or Gordo or the past incarnate come back to mow me down.

"What happened in North Carolina?" I keep both hands on the wheel and my eyes on the approaching vehicle.

Lina tenses too. Like we're both waiting for the other shoe to drop right on us. "It took my mom a couple of months to find another loser boyfriend who blew most of her blood money on meth and backhanded me whenever I gave him a piece of my mind. Once I stopped feeling numb, I realized I was angry as hell. At him. At my mom. At Gerry. But mostly, at myself. I petitioned the court for emancipation, and I've been on my own ever since."

When the truck zips past, leaving us alone again, I release a shaky breath into the silence. "Doing what?"

"Plotting my revenge. And looking for you."

CHAPTER 19

SEVEN YEARS EARLIER
SIDNEY

The elevator door parted to the chandeliered lobby of the Beverly Wilshire. Sidney picked herself up from the floor, wiped her eyes, and tucked the copy of the lurid photograph into her purse, along with the check that made her feel complicit somehow.

She hurried to a nearby bathroom to compose herself. A cold splash of water to her face made her feel halfway human again. She reminded herself she'd done nothing wrong, but Gordo forced his way into her head, calling her a naughty girl. Teddy had warned her they should be discrete about dating. That the other paralegals might start to talk. Accuse her of sleeping her way to the top. And what had she done? Left the window wide open.

As Sidney headed for the exit, the elevator dinged behind her. Ducking behind a pillar, she watched the girl from Blackstone's room cross the lobby, looking like a high school student in blue jeans, Converse sneakers, and a fuzzy pink turtleneck sweater. Sidney's instincts had been spot on.

Before she could talk herself out of it, Sidney started off after the girl, following at a distance as the girl hurried from the hotel and turned left onto Wilshire Boulevard. She walked with a purpose, a swagger. Didn't slow, didn't stop, until she made another left onto Spalding Drive.

Sidney guessed her destination. The Beverly Hills High School tennis courts had already come into view, where two more girls loitered. They wore short cocktail dresses and ridiculously high heels.

As a black limousine approached, Sidney dropped back, taking a few photos with her cell. The limousine stopped for a moment, idling before the back door opened. A man got out, speaking to the girls, laughing. Sidney kept snapping pictures, even with her heart in her throat, until the limousine pulled away, leaving Blackstone's *assistant* there alone.

"Hey!" Sidney stumbled out of her hiding place and called to the girl left behind, asking the question she'd already answered for herself. "Who was that guy?"

Sidney had recognized the man. Knew him on sight. She worked for him. She'd broken bread with him. Worst of all, she'd fallen in love with his son.

"And who the hell are you?" Then as Sidney came closer, "Oh. You're the nosy bitch from the hotel. I did you a favor, you know? Getting Gerry off your back."

Wincing, Sidney could only nod.

"You really shouldn't be here. He's not the kind of guy you want to mess with."

"Yeah. He made that clear." She suddenly felt outmatched by a teenager. "But you're not his assistant. You barely look sixteen."

The girl laughed, cocking her head at Sidney as she started to walk back toward the hotel. "No shit, Sherlock," she called over her shoulder. "That's because I'm fifteen. And if I see you again, Gerry will know about it."

As soon as the girl had vanished, Sidney dialed Teddy's number, unsure what to say. Fifteen? She felt sick. The whole afternoon had turned into a waking dream, a nightmare that bled into the day.

"Hey, beautiful. I had fun last—"

"Where's your dad right now?"

"Uh . . . he left work early. He's got some friends in town."

"Friends?"

"I don't know, Sid. You're acting weird. Why does it matter?"

Sidney sighed. "It doesn't. It doesn't matter at all."

****

Gerald Blackstone had some nerve. Sidney sat at her desk, seething as she tried to drown out his obnoxious voice, audible even with her door closed.

When she'd arrived back at Calypso headquarters, Blackstone had commandeered the office across from her own. At the desk, Mollie Jenkins, another blonde-haired, blue-eyed Drucker and Webber paralegal who seemed to fawn over his every word. Well, good for her.

Sidney planned on doing exactly nothing. Let Blackstone fire her. She'd be better off for it. After gathering the files for the expansion, she stacked them in a banker's box near the door. Then she picked up the office phone to call Mollie, pressing the button for an open line. If Mollie wanted the job, she could have it. Leaning tower of files included.

Before Sidney could dial, she heard an unfamiliar voice through the receiver.

"Mr. Blackstone, this is James McHenry calling from the Bank of Grand Cayman with your password request. We understand you believe your account details may have been compromised."

"Rogue employee," Blackstone answered as Sidney held her breath. "It's probably nothing but just to be safe . . ."

"Of course. Your account security is our priority. With that in mind, I want to remind you of our strict instructions. Memorize your nine-digit code. We strongly recommend you don't share or document it in any way, sir. Are you ready?"

Sidney nodded to herself, grabbing a pen and a Post-it. Though she had no clue what to do with the Errinyes account password, just knowing she had it—that she'd swiped it right under Blackstone's nose—felt like a small victory. Her ace in the hole, she slid it in her pocket, ready to play it at the right time.

CHAPTER 20

THURSDAY MORNING
MIDNIGHT
COVINGTON HOUSE

Lina reads the directions off the screen of the burner cell like I don't know the way to Covington House by heart. Even after seven years, I could drive the winding route of Loma Vista Drive with my eyes closed. Snaking through the heart of Beverly Hills, it leads back to ground zero. To the gardens where I last held Sidney. To my father's study where he drew his final breath.

When I see its elegant lines bisecting the sky, its bones rising on the hillside and backlit by the moon, I take in a breath. That house is the beginning and end of everything. Which is why I'd promised Lina twenty-five miles ago that the key would be here.

On my last night as Teddy Drucker, I'd returned to Covington House. My father had been dead for weeks, but the locks remained unchanged. His estate, still unsettled, with Tanya predictably insisting she should inherit the mansion, even though she spent all her time at the Spire. I'd downed the remnants of the fifth of vodka my father kept hidden in his desk drawer and wandered into the gardens, drunk and morose. But I'd sobered up fast the moment I saw the shadowy figure, unmoving between the rose bushes. I'd called out for Sidney, a hopeful ache cracking my heart. As if she'd still be there, waiting for me to save her. I'd crept toward the shadow, finding a newly erected bronze statue of the scales of justice.

"Earth to Trevor."

Startled by Lina's voice, I slam the brakes.

"You drove right past the gate."

"Shit. Sorry." I pull over to the curb, still a million miles away. "Probably better if we park here anyway."

Lina studies me in the dome light. "Are you alright?"

I nod, watching the dash clock advance one minute. 12:02 a.m. "I'm fine."

"Well, you need to be better than fine. We're about to break into a historical landmark. I need you on your A game." Lina cracks the passenger door, putting one foot on the pavement before she glances back over her shoulder. "Paige needs you."

With that, I step out of the sedan to face my past. Towering over us, cold and monstrous, its secrets well hidden behind the dark bay windows, the tall wrought-iron gate.

I secure the straps of the go-bag over my shoulders like a backpack, in preparation for a hasty getaway, and follow Lina up the tree-lined street.

"Do you know Latin?" I ask her, trying to silence the chatter in my head. To stop the memories unspooling like a runaway film reel.

"Latin? What do you think? They teach that crap in private school." She waits for me to explain.

I say, simply, "I think I know where to find the last piece of the key."

Lina and I loop the perimeter of Covington House, spotting the cameras installed at the front and back gates. The unnerving silence raises the hairs on the back of my neck, but I prefer it to the occasional bark of a dog in the distance. That dissonant note of warning sends my heart scampering every time, my hand reaching for the butt of the gun in my waistband.

I lead Lina to the side of the house, adjacent to the gardens, and stand there like it's not just after midnight. Like we're not about to break in. Like it's any other Thursday.

"What's your plan?" Lina asks.

"We could wait till morning. Sneak off during the 8 a.m. tour."

"Seriously?"

I look up at the stone privacy fence with dread, half tempted to turn around. It's not the fence itself—I'd scaled it more than a dozen times in high school, sneaking in like I had the kind of dad who noticed when I came home late—or the cameras or the alarms. It's knowing I'm a stone's throw from the garden, from the safe. From the truth.

"C'mon." I drop to one knee and extend my hand to Lina, offering her a boost. "You first."

She cocks her head at me, wedging the toe of her boot into the rockface and then hoisting herself up and over.

"Show off," I mutter, before doing the same. I drop down into the lush, wet grass, grateful that no alarm sounds, and reorient myself to the Covington House gardens. The scenic backdrop of my worst nightmares. Being here again, it's like pressing a bruise, picking at a scab that will never heal.

The hedge maze begins in the northern most corner of the lawn. Winding round and round to the elaborate stone fountain at its center, it deposits successful puzzlers in the rose garden and statuary.

Putting a finger to my lips, I take Lina's hand and lead her into the maze. The moon lights the pebbled path, casting shadows in the corners. I stay focused on Lina, her palm cool and damp in mine. It helps to keep me grounded, to stop my mind from playing tricks.

Like no time has passed, I remember the way through. Right, right, left, and right, and the center unfolds before us. The fountain, quiet now, still enchants with its four wild horses rising from the koi pond. Overlooking it, the stone bench where the legendary Clark Gable had stolen a kiss.

"Wow," Lina whispers. "I still can't believe you grew up here."

But I keep moving, tugging her along with me. The longer we stay, the heavier the chains of the past. They threaten to hold me here forever.

Another two lefts, and we pass the garden gnome Sidney loved, his red clay hat visible beneath the hedge. That night she'd rubbed it for luck. On this night, I stay as far away from it as I can manage. With luck like that, I'll take no luck at all.

Finally, the maze spits us out among the roses, though the flowers won't bloom for another few months. "We're close," I say, hoping I'm not wrong. Hoping it's still here, the way my father left it. I skirt between the thorny bushes, searching the statues. "There." I point Lina to the elegant stone woman, her eyes blindfolded. In one hand, she holds the scales. In the other, the sword. "Before my father died, he commissioned this statue."

My heart pounds in my throat when I kneel at the base of the statue where a small plaque rests in the earth like a gravestone. Lina joins me there, brushing the dirt from it.

"*Fiat justitia, ruat caelum.*" She stumbles through the Latin phrase. "Interpret please."

"Let justice be done, though the heavens fall."

"Damn, Trevor."

"I know. It must mean something, right?"

Lina sinks her fingers into the earth and starts digging.

Forty-five minutes later, Lina collapses back onto the grass, breathing heavy from the effort, though we have nothing to show for it. Only filthy hands and dirt caked beneath our fingernails.

"We have to keep digging." I push a pile of damp earth to the side and bear down deeper into the soil. My fingers ache. Sweat drips from my nose. But I can't stop. I won't.

Shaking her head in disgust, Lina rises to her feet. "There's nothing here. It's over."

"Don't say that. We still have time to keep looking." I refocus my efforts, certain it must be here, buried deep. Because I need it to be.

"Justice." Lina spits out the word like a bitter seed. "There's no justice for men like Blackstone. There never will be. Not as long as there are girls like me, desperate for somebody to notice them. And guys like him, taking whatever they want—*whoever*—and feeling entitled to it." She palms a small stone from a nearby planter. Before I can stop her, she rears back and hurls it at the head of the statue. It ricochets off Lady Justice, landing somewhere in the rose bed.

"Lina—"

"Sorry. I'm just so—"

"Do that again," I tell her, jabbing my finger at the statue.

I'm sure she thinks I'm crazy. Maybe I am. But when she pitches another stone at the statue, I hear it. Not a clunk or a thud but a delicate ping. Like the soft ringing of a bell.

I spring to my feet for a closer examination, thumping my fingernail against the statue from bottom to top. When I reach the head, the sound changes. "It's hollow."

"Do you think the last piece of the key could be inside?" Lina asks.

I shrug. "It's worth a shot."

Climbing onto the statue's small base, I inspect the smooth curve of Lady Justice's neck. There's a fine crack—barely discernible—in the welding. With the bronze cold as ice beneath my fingers, I seize hold of her face, trying to budge the head one way or the other. Lina joins me on the other side, placing her hands on mine. Together, we wrestle and tug and grunt, stopping only to expel a frustrated breath.

Finally, with my forearms cramping, I let go and stumble back down onto the grass, defeated. My blood boils at the thought that my father wanted it this way. Me, scrambling to figure him out the way I'd always done—while Paige's life hangs in the balance.

"This is crazy," I mutter.

But Lina keeps toiling. Her cheeks turn ruddy. Her dark hair clings, wet against her forehead. Behind her, the house watches, indifferent.

While I lay there feeling sorry for myself, my eyes are drawn to a glint beneath the rose bush. A hand trowel forgotten by the gardener.

"Hey, I've got an idea."

I grab the trowel and the largest stone I can find, making my way back to the statue and to Lina. I position the edge of the small shovel inside the crack and strike the handle with the stone. Once, twice, three times.

Lina reaches for my hand, meets my eyes. "It's loose," she says.

I swallow a lump and nod at her, then she gives it a hard twist and pull. The head of Lady Justice rests in Lina's hands.

Wide-eyed, Lina beckons me over. My stomach flip-flops like a fish out of water, but I walk to her anyway. She holds the head steady in the moonlight while I peer at the tiny brown envelope affixed to the underside.

Neither of us speak. I reach in and remove it, unfolding the flap and dumping the contents into my palm.

While I stare dumbfounded at my shaking hand, Lina produces the pendants from her pocket. She holds them up to me.

"Look. It's a match."

Though the third piece isn't attached to a chain like the others, it's made of the same antique metal, with an identical row of gemstones. Ruby and black jade, the color of playing cards. My father's winning hand.

CHAPTER 21

SEVEN YEARS EARLIER
TEDDY

Teddy groaned as he stepped over another coiled string of Christmas lights in the foyer of Covington House. With one week to go, his father had ramped up the preparations for the annual holiday party. This year, like every year before it, had to be bigger, better, and more lavish than the last. Which had never made sense to Teddy, given his father's disdain for anything festive or sentimental. But then Alan Drucker never missed an opportunity to boost his ego.

At least Teddy had a date this year. He wouldn't have to make pretend small talk or kiss the asses of his father's cronies all night. Instead, he would turn heads with Sidney on his arm.

Retrieving his Berluti briefcase from the hall closet, Teddy paused at the front door, turning for one last look. Clad in its disguise of freshly cut pine trees draped in twinkling lights, red velvet bows tied on the banister, Covington House looked like a home.

"Oh good, you're still here." His father descended the stairs in his usual uniform. Black Zegna suit, suede Ferragamo loafers, and a perfectly knotted silk tie. "Could you check in with Gerry today? I want to make sure he's satisfied with the new paralegal."

Teddy blinked in surprise. "New paralegal? I thought Sidney was assigned to the Calypso account. Gerry wanted it that way."

"Changed his mind, apparently." With a heavy sigh, his father took hold of his own, larger, briefcase and led Teddy out the door to the waiting driver. "As of yesterday, Sidney's been removed from the account. Didn't she tell you?"

"Of course. It's been so hectic at the office, I forgot."

"Sure you did."

Teddy watched, speechless, while his dad climbed into the back seat. He couldn't let on that Sidney had told him exactly nothing. That she'd been acting strangely for days now, ever since she'd phoned him to ask about his father's whereabouts.

"Best nip that in the bud, son. If a woman lies to you when you're dating, she sure as hell won't tell you the truth after you put a rock on her finger and half your assets in her name."

Though his father's hypocrisy scraped at his insides, he nodded his agreement.

"Can I get a ride with you?" Teddy asked, already dreading the commute. Even his fully loaded Benz didn't help ease the strain of bumper-to-bumper traffic.

His father didn't look up from his cellphone. "You know I like my peace and quiet in the morning. I'll see you at the office."

****

Teddy didn't go to the office. Because fuck Alan Drucker and his driver and his stupid peace and quiet. Instead, he drove to Sidney's apartment in Venice Beach, his fury tightening into a hot ball at the center of his stomach. By the time he arrived, it ached.

He waited on the sidewalk, half of him hoping she'd already gone to work. The other half, desperate to give her a piece of his mind. To anyone, really.

When she strode out the front door of the building, he teetered on the verge of explosion. Because fuck her and her sexy shirtdress and the smile she flashed that he knew he didn't deserve. Never mind the flatness in her eyes, the dark circles.

"Why didn't you tell me that Blackstone had a problem with you? You know you can come to me. You should've come to me. I am the Senior Client Relations Manager." His voice grew in strength as he spoke, and a few passersby craned their heads to look at the crazy man he'd turned into.

"I tried. I really did."

"Bullshit."

"Why are you yelling?"

"I'm not yelling."

Sidney's bottom lip trembled. Behind her hand, he watched her face crumple like a used tissue. But he didn't comfort her.

"I'm glad I'm not on the account anymore," she said. "And if you cared about me at all, you would be too. Blackstone is a crook, Teddy. He's dangerous, and I never want to see—"

The ring of Teddy's cell in his pocket shut her up. "Restricted number."

"Go ahead," she told him. "Answer it."

Teddy held the phone to his ear while Sidney stood there crying.

"Collect call from an inmate at Los Angeles County Jail. Do you accept the charges?"

Head spinning, blood still pumping too fast, Teddy muttered, "Yes."

****

Eight hours later, Teddy loaded a disgraced Alan Drucker into the passenger seat of his Benz as the cameras flashed around them. At the arraignment, his father had pronounced himself not guilty and walked free after posting a meager twenty-thousand-dollar bail.

"What the hell is going on, Dad?"

Predictably, his father said nothing. Then, "You were there. You heard the judge. You know as much as I do."

"Really? That's it? That's all you have to say for yourself?"

"It's been the longest day of my life, Teddy. Lay off it."

"Longest day of *your* life?" Teddy squeezed the wheel so tight, his hands hurt. He could barely see the road through his blurry eyes. "You owe me an explanation. And what about Tanya? She's going to freak."

"Tanya will be fine. She knows how women are. They'll say anything if the price is right."

"The cops have photos, Dad. They have surveillance video. They have victims—young girls—willing to testify."

According to Jordy Webber, his father's law firm partner and newly appointed attorney, Alan Drucker and Gerald Blackstone had been the subjects of an anonymous tip that led to a weeklong investigation into the prostitution of underage girls at the Beverly Wilshire Hotel. Both men had been arrested publicly outside their offices that morning. A spectacle that would, no doubt, grace the front page of the *LA Times* tomorrow morning.

"Victims?" His father scoffed. "You know how it is with women these days. The way they dress, the way they talk. You can hardly tell how old they are."

Teddy stared straight ahead, wishing he could disappear. He thought of Sidney, how she'd comforted him, even after he'd acted like a total ass. Maybe she'd let him spend the night.

"Did you do it? Did you have sex with those girls?"

His father reared back as if Teddy had slapped him. "You're always missing the goddamn point. Someone is out to ruin me. To destroy everything I've built. I've got a target on my back. And I need you on my side."

"I'll take that as a yes, then."

CHAPTER 22

THURSDAY MORNING 1 A.M. COVINGTON HOUSE

Taking the antique pendant between my fingers, I separate the top portion and pass it to Lina. It snaps into place, magnetized alongside the others, to form a complete rectangle.

She gapes at it for a moment, awestruck. "This is it. The key. Now we just need the place to put it."

She points up at the house, to the dark windows overlooking the gardens. The perennial morning glory winding about the trellis, creeping up the stone. I imagine the ghosts who live there—my father, Sidney—waiting to bind me with their chains, but I've come too far to turn back. I nod my agreement.

"The second floor," I whisper. "That's how we get in."

Holding the wrought-iron trellis with one hand, Lina frowns at me, her skepticism writ large across her face.

"Teddy Drucker scaled this trellis," I assure her. Though I only did it the once. On a dare. At sixteen. And I can still hear the snap of my left wrist, clean as the break of a rose's stem, when I tumbled from it.

"Well, Teddy Drucker was an idiot."

"Touché." I start to climb, already nervous about maintaining a firm grip with my sweaty palms. About the rough vines scraping my skin. And the long and pitiful fall to earth, especially with the weight of the go-bag on my back. "But Dad never alarmed the crow's nest window. It's our best shot."

Lina follows alongside me, hand over hand on the cold iron, both of us too careful to speak. I don't dare look down for fear I'll see the fires of hell below me, Sidney laughing as I plummet and burn. After what I've done, it's the least I deserve.

I secure my foot in the next hold, reaching upward. Suddenly, my stomach bottoms out as my foot slips from beneath me, leaving me hanging, face down in the vines.

Lina smirks at me from above. "You alright, Spiderman?"

Taking a quick breath, I manage to return my feet to safety. After a few more cautious steps, we reach the shingled roof.

Grateful for the cover of darkness, I scramble up to the crow's nest with Lina behind me. I perch there, my fingers searching for a grip beneath the window's frame. Behind it, the gossamer curtains hide the room that once held the Drucker family's sparse memories. My father's old law books. My high school graduation cap and gown. Not a trace of my mother, though. She'd been erased and replaced, like all the women who'd come after her.

"Moment of truth." I tug upward, muscling the pane open. The movement sends a shiver of wind through the curtains, but the house remains mercifully silent.

I swing one leg over the sill and step inside, before I help Lina through. As my eyes adjust to the pitch-black, the unfinished attic of my childhood reveals itself to be a lot like me. Unchanged in all the ways that matter.

Dusty boxes line the hardwood. A few of them remain open, displaying the museum's collection of old movie props, memorabilia, and Gatsby-themed party décor. A single string still dangles from the bare bulb at the center. Tempting, but I don't dare. I turn to Lina, still in disbelief, and huff out a quiet laugh at our luck.

When my gaze follows Lina's to the far corner, I freeze. A dark figure stands in judgment, ready to strike. I fumble for the gun at my waist, pointing it at the silhouette. I hold my aim steady until Lina cracks a smile.

"It's only a mannequin," she says, giving the figure a little push. "You should probably put that thing away. Before someone real gets hurt."

The figure topples to the side. Its plastic head rests against the wall, while its blank eyes mock me from beneath a Flapper-era headband. Behind it, a horde of them stand upright, stoic, clad in beaded fringe dresses. Laying alongside their slim, posed legs, a glittery sign that reads HAPPY NEW YEAR!

"C'mon." I try to save face, returning the Glock to the go-bag and tugging Lina past the mannequin army toward the door. "We don't have time to mess around."

She trails me down the winding staircase from the crow's nest toward the second floor and the ornate oak door that leads to my father's old study. Further down the dark hall is the lonely room that belonged to Teddy Drucker. Memories will sink me faster than quicksand, so I keep focused.

The knob feels cold beneath my fingers. As if it hasn't been touched in years. As if my dead father might still be inside, waiting for me to join him. Casting my fears aside, I thrust it open and peer into the inky cave.

The moonlight seeps in between the curtains of the corner window illuminating all that's gone. My father, for starters. The room looks strangely empty without him in it. His executive desk, with its cherrywood veneer and Greek column motifs on all four corners. The ergonomic chair he'd paid through the nose for. All of it, vanished. The bookcases, the wood-burning fireplace, and the freshly polished hardwood floor are all that remain. As I make my way across it, the hollow sound of my footsteps unnerves me.

"Do you remember how to open it?" Lina asks.

I nod, unloading the go-bag and dropping to one knee on the hearth fashioned from river stone. Reaching alongside the firebox, I find the smooth gray rock with a point at one end. I take a breath before I wrap my hands around its edges and pull, then wait for the audible click from the center bookcase.

Lina gives one end a gentle push and gasps when it parts from the rest of the wall, revealing the room behind it. "It's here," she mouths, almost disbelieving. "It's still here."

I stand at the entrance, staring into the dark space. It's like a tomb, cold and musty, and I shiver as I step inside. For the first time since we entered the crow's nest, I turn on a light, flinching beneath its brightness. Like a monstrous beast, the safe hulks at the center of the barren room, at least six feet of solid steel bolted to the floor. The small desk and metal chair beside it feel like a silly afterthought, dwarfed by its presence.

Lina digs into her pocket and fits together the three rectangular pendants that form the key. She holds it out to me. "You should do it."

My gut churning, I take the key in my hand and find the slot above the spoke handle. Gently, carefully, I slide the key inside, feeling Lina's wary gaze on my back.

Moments later, the safe emits an electronic chirp. Seizing the handle, I pull it open before I can change my mind.

Neither of us speak. The shelves are bare. No cash. No jewelry. No human remains. The only item inside—a plain brown envelope—rests on the middle shelf.

There's no writing on it. No name or instruction. The foolish hope that's clung to me all these years like sea smoke, that my father might have left something behind for me, disappears to nothing.

I peer into the envelope and count two flash drives. They appear identical, except for the minor detail that nearly breaks me. The letters *S.A.* written in marker. I imagine my father doodling it himself, penning Sidney's initials on one of the drives.

Raising my eyes to Lina's, I point her back to the study. "Get the laptop from the duffel."

As soon as she disappears, I empty the envelope onto the desk. The flash drives clatter onto its surface. Cold and sterile and disappointing. Fitting, I think, that these, of all things, are Alan Drucker's hidden treasure. Before Lina returns, I slip the uniquely marked drive into the pocket of my jeans. Whatever happened to Sidney, it stays with me. For my eyes only.

"Are you sure you want to do this now?" Lina sets the laptop in front of me. "Here?"

I take a seat on the chair and consider the remaining drive. "I have to know. I have to see what's there."

"Sometimes, you're better off not knowing. There are some things you can't unsee, Trevor."

Ignoring Lina's warning, I fit the drive into the USB port. On the screen, a password prompt appears.

"Lolita," Lina says, reluctantly.

"Of course it is." My insides twist with each keystroke.

A list of files unfurls down the screen, most of them titled "Errinyes Financial Statement" and marked with a date ranging from seven to ten years ago. I select the most recent and open it. A warning message appears.

READ ONLY. File cannot be copied or transmitted.

"Damn," I mutter, though it's not surprising. "What's Errinyes? I've never heard of it."

Lina sighs over my shoulder. "That's the blackmail money. Blackstone used Errinyes Realty to hide his ill-gotten gains."

I open a file at random, finding a list of client numbers and moneys received, most of them upwards of $25,000. Lina puts her finger on the screen, pointing to Client 39 and his substantial payments. "That's Senator Crawley."

My mouth, sandpaper dry, I keep scrolling to the MP4 video files. Lina paces behind me, her breathing as shallow as mine.

Even though she'd prepared me for it, I gape at the hundred or so file names. By the time I reach the bottom, I count at least five congressmen and two senators, including Crawley. A software mogul, an Oscar-winning actor, a Fortune 500 CEO. Professional athletes too.

"Are these what I think they are?"

Lina nods, her expression unreadable. To be honest, I'm surprised she's holding up this well. The girl who sat on my couch for the last eight weeks would be a puddle by now.

"His insurance policies. Blackstone insisted that all his girls film at least one encounter for each of his clients. He'd take the men out on his yacht. Tell them, anything goes. It's all legal in international waters. They had no idea he had cameras in all the bedrooms."

Disgusted, I stare at the screen until my eyes burn. "We should go." I feel the sudden urge to run. To leave the Lolita files behind. To get as far from Covington House as I can and never look back. "We've been here too long."

But Lina stops me. Her mouth hangs slightly open, the glow from the screen illuminating the dark circles beneath her eyes. She raises her hand, her index finger poised and ready. It lingers for a moment—like she's making up her mind—before she sets it on the final file on the list, last modified seven years ago, late December.

"That could be it. The snuff film. The date looks about right."

"Are you sure you want to watch it?" I ask.

Without answering, Lina reaches over me and summons the past with a click of her finger on the touch pad. I gape at the ghost on the screen.

If you're watching this, there's a good chance I'm dead. Or in prison.

My father speaks directly to the camera, flashes that smart-ass smirk, and for a moment, it's as if he never left.

Same difference if you ask me. You know I wouldn't last a day in San Quentin, Teddy.

I gulp at his pixelated image. Behind him, the gray walls of this very room cast him in shadow.

I lost my way, I'll admit it. I let you down. But I never thought it would go this far. I never thought Gerry would take a life. Forgive me, son. For all I've done. For all I've failed to do. You're a better man than me. Don't make the same mistakes I did. You have the ammunition here to end him. Do the right thing.

"Trevor?" Lina lays a hand on my shoulder.

I register her touch, even if I'm gone, floating off somewhere a million miles away. Somewhere where the past can't hurt me.

"You heard your dad. *Gerry took a life.* That film has to be here somewhere."

"Well, we don't have time to look for it," I say, too quickly. "We have what we came for. Let's get the hell out of here."

"You just don't get it, do you?"

The accusatory tone in Lina's voice grates. Probably it's my guilty conscience playing tricks on me, the second flash drive weighing heavy in my pocket.

I rush to close the file, relieved when the computer screen goes blank. "Get what?"

"The reason I need the files. The reason I was willing to risk everything to get them." She paces from one end of the small room to the other, suddenly spinning in my direction. "We can't turn them over to Gordo and Blackstone. We have to go to the cops, Trevor. To the media. If we don't, he wins. And a guy like that never stops winning."

I pull the flash drive from the port and toss it onto the table, marveling at how something so ordinary can hold such devastation. "But what about Paige? If we expose Blackstone, she's as good as dead. And you know I'll take the fall for it. Blackstone will make sure of that. We have to follow through with the plan. After that, you can do what you want."

Lina surprises me when she doesn't argue. She joins me at the table instead, resigned.

"I can't bring Sidney back, but I can still save Paige. We can save her. That should count for something." Overwhelmed, I lay my head in my hands. But that's no good. Because Sidney's image appears in the dark space behind my eyes. The last helpless look she'd levied at me.

A soft sound breaks through my reverie. When I raise my head, Lina stands at the bookcase door, looking strangely satisfied. "Save her yourself. I'm going to give Blackstone what he deserves."

"Wait."

Before I can stop her, Lina steps through the opening, shutting me inside. I spring up from the chair and push on the edge of the hidden door, yelling her name. When it doesn't budge, the room starts to close in around me. Trying to still my ragged breathing, I spin back toward the desk and find it bare. She's taken the flash drive with her.

CHAPTER 23

SEVEN YEARS EARLIER
TEDDY

Alan Drucker never got sick. Sometimes Teddy wondered if his father really had struck a deal with the devil. Despite his steady diet of red meat and sugar and hard liquor, his father seemed to have the stamina of a racehorse. A racehorse with a paunch, but still.

"I don't buy it, Dad. You're avoiding people. Just admit it. I wouldn't blame you."

From the confines of his bed, his father responded with a cough so dramatic Teddy hoped he hadn't pulled a muscle. "I'm not avoiding anything. The doctor said it's best for me to get my rest. Besides, I don't want to expose anyone at the party to whatever this is."

"Then maybe we should cancel. What am I supposed to say?"

"You know we can't cancel now, Teddy. Go and enjoy yourself. I invited that waitress you liked from the Marmont. Once she sees this place, I'll bet you she puts out."

Teddy marveled at the way his dad could make him feel so small. The way he had no shame, no matter what he'd done. Truly, the man had skills.

"I hope you didn't tell her to look for me. Sidney is my date for the party. Sidney is my girlfriend."

His father groaned. "I thought we covered this. That bitch is not welcome in this house. You know what she's done to me. To this family. She has no loyalty. Not to you. Not to me. Not to anyone but herself."

"You don't know her like I do. She'd never call the cops on you or Gerry. She would come to me first."

"Don't kid yourself, son. She's got you figured for a pussy-whipped sap. Which half the damn time, you are. Sometimes I wonder if I made life too easy for you. Maybe I should've given Nick the corner office. At least he would've appreciated it."

No sooner had the sting wore off from one barb, his father unleased another. "Now I'm not so mean that I'd fire Sidney before Christmas, but come the New Year, she's out on her ass. And if you know what's good for you, you'll let her give you one last shag, and then you'll tell her goodbye."

Teddy shifted side to side, trying to work up the nerve to tell his father to stick it. Instead, he muttered, "Hope you feel better," all the while, secretly, silently, wishing Alan Drucker dead.

****

"Are you sure you're ready for this?" Teddy stood outside his front door, feeling like an outsider. "We can still bail on the party and spend the night at your house watching cheesy Christmas movies."

"I'm ready." Sidney held tight to his arm and smiled up at him. "You?"

Teddy didn't want to be there at all. But Sidney had insisted, reminding him that his father's mistakes didn't matter to her. That he had no reason to hide his face. When she'd sent him the photo of herself, posing in front of her mirror, he couldn't say no. Because her body in that red dress deserved to be seen, and the place to be seen tonight was Covington House. At the annual Drucker and Webber holiday soiree. No matter what his father said.

"Ready as I'll ever be."

As the front doors parted, Teddy nearly gasped at the sprawling crowd. Bigger than ever, even amid the worst scandal the firm had ever seen. As they entered the foyer, Teddy sensed their cutting glances, heard the chorus of their whispers following him beneath the festive music. Even strawman Nick averted his eyes, pretending he didn't see Teddy wave at him.

Teddy realized, then, that he stood smack dab in the middle of a head-on collision. These rubberneckers couldn't tear their eyes away from the carnage. They hadn't shown up despite it, but because of it. No wonder his father had insisted on staying holed up in the master bedroom on the second floor.

Downing a glass of champagne from a server's tray, Sidney tugged him toward the dance floor. "It's just you and me," she said. "Forget about them."

Teddy surrendered and pulled her close, swaying to the beat. But his father's warning drowned out the music. Since Blackstone's arrest, Sidney did seem newly liberated. He couldn't blame her after the prick had dismissed her from the Calypso account for no good reason. Still, people talk, and rumblings in the office had pointed to Sidney as the anonymous tipper. As far as Teddy could tell, neither Gerry nor his father had the balls to ask her straight up.

When the song neared its crescendo, Sidney twirled at the end of his hand, radiant. Her dress spun around her. Her blonde hair caught the light. She looked like a Christmas angel. Suddenly, she stopped, her eyes fixed behind him.

"You should be in a movie, Ms. Archer."

Teddy recognized the voice before he turned toward it.

"That dress really is something, isn't it?" Blackstone's gaze roamed Sidney's body, making Teddy blush. "Who's the designer?"

Sidney stepped to Teddy's side, facing Blackstone in his perfectly tailored tux. Her head lifted, chin jutted in challenge.

"Actually, I bought it for fifty bucks at a thrift store downtown. Designer clothes are so overrated. Now, if you'll excuse me . . ."

Teddy started to follow her, eager to wriggle free of Blackstone's attention. But the man stopped him with a hand to his chest. "I'm surprised you'd bring her here after what she's done to your family."

Teddy wanted to counter, *I'm surprised you'd even show your face*, but found the words stuck in his throat when he saw Blackstone's body man, Gordo, lingering in the corner. Teddy hardly knew him, but the guy had a reputation for busting heads. He fluttered his fingers at Teddy in an obnoxious wave.

"Do you want your father to go to prison?"

"Of course not." But Teddy wasn't entirely sure that was the whole truth. Mostly, he wanted his father gone but not what came with it. The lengthy trial. His inheritance, drained. The complete and utter humiliation.

"Then you need to work with us to get to the bottom of this. We just want to talk to her, find out what she knows."

"How am I supposed to help with that?"

Blackstone grinned, slapped him on the back so hard Teddy's teeth juddered. "Bring her to the center of the hedge maze at midnight. Gordo will handle it from there."

CHAPTER 24

THURSDAY MORNING
2 A.M.
COVINGTON HOUSE

With Lina gone rogue, vanished with the flash drive, I brace myself against the wall of my father's hidden room and summon Doctor Trevor Dent. He's still in here, buried under the rubble with his PhD and his scented candles and his guided meditation scripts.

I breathe. In through the nose. Out through the mouth.

Lina, gone!

I pick a point. Focus on it. Try to stay in the present moment.

Flash drive, gone!

I search for a happy memory. Try to think of a funny joke to tell myself. But all roads lead me here. Trapped in a box with no escape.

God knows what else she's swiped from the go-bag.

I smack my palm against the wall, which hurts like hell and does exactly nothing to help my situation. I can't even blame Lina for the mess I'm in. Though I'll admit, her leaving me high and dry stings worse than I thought it would.

Letting my legs fold beneath me, I sink to the floor and close my eyes, taking slow breaths until I finally bring the racehorse in my chest back to a steady trot. I remember my father, addressing the camera alone. In the video, three of the room's four walls had been visible, telling me that he'd likely been locked inside himself.

There must be a way out.

Scanning each partition, I come up empty. I make my way around the safe to the back wall and search from floor to ceiling. I finally spot it on the baseboard, just near the seams of the bookcase door. I'd been flying blind, my brain too doused in adrenaline to notice.

When I push the button, the bookcase parts from the wall, and I rush out of the office. My worst fears confirmed, the go-bag gapes open. The gun, missing. I grab the bag anyway and hurry toward freedom. As I reach the landing, I hear Lina below me, fumbling with the front door's lock.

"Lina, stop!" I call to her, more desperate this time. But it's too late. She flings open the door, and the alarm blares, taking an ax blade to the quiet.

I bound down two flights of stairs and out the open door into the early morning, watching while Lina disappears behind the gate. She won't get far without the car key. I touch my pocket, reassuring myself.

Lugging the duffel bag over my shoulder, I follow behind her. My eyes dart to the silhouette in the lit window of the house next door, certain it's the alarm that's roused the neighbor. The signal still wails behind me, growing fainter the farther I travel down the sidewalk.

Two blocks ahead, Lina picks up her pace, tucking the Glock beneath her jacket as she passes our sedan.

A pair of headlights turns the corner, momentarily blinding me. I take cover behind the nearest tree, but it's too late for Lina. She's been spotted.

The incoming SUV rumbles onto the sidewalk and screeches to a stop, blocking Lina's path. When the passenger window slides down, she raises her hands in surrender.

"Going somewhere?" Gordo asks her.

From my hiding place, I can't make out a weapon but the terror on Lina's face, spotlighted by the street lamp, seems proof enough. The gun she swiped from my go-bag stays hidden.

"Back to the car. I need to get—"

"Stop talking." Gordo leans his head out and I duck back, afraid he's spotted me. A guy like that can smell fear. "I warned Gerry about you. I told him from the beginning that we couldn't trust you. That you would try to double-cross us, sell the files to the highest bidder. You're lucky Gerry's got a hard-on for you that just won't quit. Otherwise, you'd be dead by now. Hand them over, Lina."

Though I'm standing stock-still, the solid ground slips out from beneath me, sending me into a freefall. The alarm at Covington House continues to bleat its panicked warning, but I can hardly hear it over the white noise in my head. Over the crushing sound of betrayal that takes me back to that night, to the gardens with Sidney.

"I don't know what you're talking about," Lina says.

"You always were a bad liar when it counted." Then Gordo extends his arm through the window, the gun visible and pointed right at her. "You're out of options, sweetheart. Don't make me get out of the car. You won't like what happens."

I hear no response, but Lina finally steps toward him, rearing back and letting the flash drive fly. It takes a single bounce on the asphalt and disappears into the dead leaves piled in the gutter.

Lina takes off running, sprinting down the sidewalk until she's out of sight. Gordo and his henchman exit the SUV, desperate to locate their precious files. I almost laugh as they paw through the detritus. But when Gordo raises his hand, victorious, my heart sinks.

After the SUV speeds past, I release a shaky breath and hurry back down the deserted street to the sedan, fumbling with the key. In my haste, it clatters against the pavement, skittering into the shadows beneath the car. I curse under my breath, taking a quick glance over my shoulder and dropping to one knee. When I extend my arm to reach for it, I squint up at the strange box affixed to the underside of the vehicle. A gentle tug, and it comes loose in my hand. One side is magnetized. The other blinks back at me with a taunting yellow light that reminds me I should have known better.

Gordo's been tracking us since Vegas, circling above vulture-like. Just waiting to swoop in and take what doesn't belong to him.

Two can play at that game.

I jog back down the street with the tracking device, affixing it beneath a moving van parked in a driveway. I head back and fire the engine. At the end of the block, I raise my eyes to the rearview, saying another goodbye. To Covington House. To Lina. To my father. No matter what happens next, it's undeniable. I am completely and utterly alone.

****

The dash clock reads 3 a.m. Darkness drapes from one end of the beach to the other. I peer out the windshield unable to tell where the sand ends and the ocean begins. Even the Pacific Wheel at Santa Monica Pier stands still, its festive bright lights illuminating the black water.

I've been parked here for exactly sixteen minutes, with the laptop open on the passenger seat. The bright screen demands my attention, though I'd rather walk to the sea and heave it in, watching it sink beneath the surface. That's what Teddy Drucker would do, content to live in blissful ignorance.

Seventeen minutes now. And I still can't bear to press play on the single video file located on the flash drive marked *S.A.* It's the only bargaining chip I've got left. The only hope of winning Paige's freedom, but I'm sure it'll break me. It already has.

It's dated three days after I delivered Sidney to Gordo in the Covington House gardens like a puppy I didn't want anymore. The first still image is a grainy shot of her frightened face.

The blood whooshes in my ears. My pulse throbs. *You're better off not knowing.* That's what Lina said. Some stones are best left unturned.

But my finger hovers over the play button. I owe a debt for what I've done. It's high time I paid up.

You're about to make history. I recognize Gordo's gravelly voice even if I can't see him beneath his dark hood. His meaty hands are all over her, petting the hair I once ran my fingers through. But worse, I recognize the other man too. Senator Crawley, creeping in the shadows. Worst of all, I can't tear my eyes from the girl in the chair.

Prickles spread across my skin in hot flashes, and I break into a cold sweat. My heart pounds now against my rib cage, demanding to be let out. And again, I wonder if I might die right here after all, like my father. Wish for it even.

Seven minutes and thirty-three seconds, the camera never strays from Sidney's face. Not when Gordo binds her hands and ankles, leaving her there unable to fend for herself. Not when the senator makes her do unspeakable things. Not even when he puts his hands around the pale white of her throat, squeezing, squeezing, squeezing until her body stills beneath him.

The senator slumps against her, exhausted. Then he struggles to his feet. Zips his pants. Straightens his clothing. Exits the room the way he came in. Like he'd ended a business meeting, not a human life. Before the video cuts out abruptly, I lose myself in the waiting, willing Sidney to take the breath that never comes.

Wiping hot tears from my face, I force myself back to the surface. Back to the here and now. Rising way too fast, I sicken like a diver with the bends. Bile creeps up the back of my throat, and I double-over, dry heaving onto the floorboard.

Senator Crawley raped and murdered Sidney, snuffing her out like a candle flame with his bare hands. And that monster Blackstone got the whole thing on video. Thank God he did. Because this is what he's after. This is *my* winning hand.

It strikes me then, a fact so strange, so horrific, I can't comprehend it. My eyes well with the ache of it. Even at the end, when death seemed an inevitable certainty, Sidney never screamed.

****

While I watch the sun come up over the Pacific Ocean, a fire boils in my belly. Steam rises from my skin. Seven years

I spent looking over my shoulder, running from the unknown. Certain the past would catch up with me, cuff me, and lock me away in a prison cell for twenty-five to life.

An LAPD detective had promised me as much. *We know you did it, Teddy, and we will prove it. We won't stop until we do. One day, you'll make some lucky cellie a pretty girlfriend.*

Seething, I open the duffel bag and take stock of what I've got left. A stack of cash and my fake ID. The computer still sits where I left it, snapped shut on the passenger seat. With the flash drive now safely tucked in my pocket, I open it again, moving it onto my lap.

I can't bring Sidney back. With the Glock gone, I can't even go out guns blazing. But I know the truth now, and the truth has power. It's a grenade, pin-pulled. A fuse, sparking.

I start typing. I begin at the beginning. I leave nothing out.

CHAPTER 25

SEVEN YEARS EARLIER
SIDNEY

Sidney hummed "Jingle Bells," as she stood in front of the downstairs bathroom mirror in Covington House, reapplying her lipstick and blotting the sheen from her forehead.

Since she'd stared into Gerry Blackstone's cold eyes three hours ago, she'd never felt freer. The thought of him spending his golden years stuck in a concrete box made her practically giddy. Even if she didn't put him there herself like he suspected, let him think it.

Though the clock neared midnight, the party showed no signs of winding down. The bright sounds of laughter and music carried through the door, calling to her. She returned her lipstick to her clutch and unlocked the door, eager to return to Teddy. He'd promised her a moonlit walk in the gardens, a kiss on the bench. A Christmas surprise.

But when she turned the knob, she met with steady resistance, and a face appeared in the crack. The girl from Blackstone's hotel room blocked her exit. She pushed Sidney back inside and turned the lock.

"What are you doing here?" Sidney asked, trying to sound brave. Clad in black trousers and a white button down, the girl appeared slightly disheveled, unhinged. Tendrils of her hair had escaped her ponytail. She wore no makeup, and the small wine stain on her shirt looked like blood. "Aren't you too young to be working the party?"

"I need to talk to you." The girl approached the sink, dabbing at the stain with a paper towel. "It's about Gerry."

Sidney nodded, watching her reflection darken. "Did he hurt you too?"

"What do you think?"

"I think there's no good reason for a fifteen-year-old girl to be wearing a bathrobe in a grown man's hotel room."

The girl's eyes teared as she rubbed the spot more vigorously. "He's going to get away with it. I don't know how. But I know he will. He'll figure it out. That I'm the one who tipped off the cops. The one who set up the sting. I'm too young to die."

"Die?" The word came out strangled.

"You have no idea what he's capable of." She let her hands drop, revealing a wet circle at the center of her chest. The stain had faded little despite her effort. "And he won't stop with me. He'll take everything from all of us girls. He never loses. He told me once that he has more money than God. That he can buy anything. Anyone."

"All of us?" Sidney repeated.

"His victims. There are at least ten prepared to testify against him."

Sidney felt buoyed by the young girl's courage. "So how can I help?"

"You can't. No one can. If he finds out the truth, it's over for me."

Sidney brushed the tendrils of blonde hair from the girl's cheeks. She looked so young when she cried. "If anyone asks, I'll tell them I'm the anonymous tipper. Blackstone already suspects me anyway."

"You'd do that? For me?"

"You're just a kid. You don't deserve any of this. Let me worry about Blackstone. I can handle him."

The girl sniffled, drying the spot on her shirt with a paper towel. "My mom says, as soon as the trial is over, we need to get the hell out of here. She's scared Blackstone's people will try to find us."

"That's probably smart." Sidney found herself surprised that the girl had a mother at all. A mother who cared enough to be afraid for her daughter. "Where will you go?"

The girl hung her head. Another tear escaped, running down her face and onto the bathroom counter. "That's the thing. We don't have any money. We can barely make the rent. Honestly, I don't know what we'll do."

Sidney thought of Blackstone. His greed, his entitlement. The wealth he'd earned on the backs of young girls like this one. She couldn't make it right, but she could make it even. "Do you have a phone? There are two numbers I want you to remember."

As the girl pecked out the numbers into the notes app on her phone, Sidney kept talking, her burden growing lighter as she spoke. "This is the account. A secret account in the Cayman Islands where he hides all the money he's not supposed to have. And this is the password. If you can get to the bank, you and your mom can take what you need and disappear. There's so much cash, he won't even notice."

The girl tucked her phone in her pocket and wrapped Sidney in a fierce hug. "Thank you," she whispered. "You have no idea how much this means."

Sidney held her for a moment, feeling the girl's heartbeat race against her chest. "Hey, I don't even know your name."

The girl looked up at her, tears dried. Her face, impossible to read. Not quite a girl, not yet a woman. "Lina."

****

Sidney found Teddy in the gardens, waiting for her. His usual boyish grin had turned serious and, for a moment, she felt a pinprick of unease. But then, he winked at her and took her by the hands, and her worries flitted away like black-winged butterflies.

"I want you to know how special you are to me." Reaching into his jacket pocket, he withdrew a small blue box, tied with a silver bow. "Open it."

Sidney tugged the lid free and lifted the pouch from inside it, removing a Sterling silver Tiffany bracelet engraved with her initials.

"Do you like it?"

"It's perfect," she said, while he slipped it on her wrist.

"Perfect like you." He leaned toward her, lips parted. But she pulled away, with a coy grin. She tossed her heels into the grass.

"Catch me." She giggled as she disappeared into the hedge maze.

CHAPTER 26

THURSDAY MORNING
4 A.M.
SHAKESPEARE BRIDGE

Too-cool-for-school Teddy Drucker never visited the Shakespeare Bridge. The only parts of LA the old me deemed worthy of exploration came with expensive price tags and Michelin stars. Fast cars, throbbing house music, and beautiful women. I'd once thumbed my nose at suburbia, but here I am smack in the middle of it.

At exactly 3:59 a.m., I leave the sedan parked near the west entrance and approach the Gothic bridge that's been deemed a city landmark. The stream that once ran beneath has long since gone dry. Instead, a lush garden blooms in its place, green even in the middle of winter. On each of its four turrets sit roofed towers, lit from within, that seem to promise enchantment not doom. The bulbs cast white halos on the concrete, shadowing the rest.

I stop at the center of the bridge and wait, gazing down at darkness below me. At the sprinkling of confetti stars above. At the ivy making its silent crawl up the pylons toward the massive archway, as a lone car whizzes past, oblivious. I take it all in. Because that's the only thing to do before you go on a suicide mission. No way Blackstone is letting me get out alive. Not after what I've seen. What I know.

As the minutes pass, I begin to doubt myself. The flash drive Gordo stole from Lina contained ample blackmail material to keep their pockets fat. Maybe Blackstone would cut his losses, satisfied. Then the paranoia sets in. Every flash of movement in the trees could be a sniper with his sight set. Once they've put a bullet in my head, they'll pluck the drive like a petal and speed away into the sunset. I crouch down, hiding behind the bridge's concrete railing.

From the west end of the bridge, a woman approaches on foot. Clad in a short skirt, high heels, and low-cut sweater, she looks out of place, underdressed for the middle of January. The nearer she comes, the clearer I see her. Not a woman at all but a girl. Her doe eyes, a dead giveaway. Her blonde hair nearly as pale as her ivory skin.

"Follow me," she says as she passes. Swinging her hips while she walks away, she stumbles a little, like a kid playing dress-up. I can't help but think of Lina. Only thirteen when she'd met Blackstone. She'd been no match for the devil.

I scramble to my feet and trail after her. But already I'm riding waves of panic, my stomach roiling and pitching like an angry sea. This isn't what I'd planned. Not who I'd planned for. Which is exactly why they'd sent her. They want to throw me off balance.

"Is Paige okay?" I hate how hopeful I sound. How naïve. "Where is she?"

The girl offers an ironic smile that doesn't reach her eyes. So it's like that. She wants to play grown-up.

"How old are you?" I ask. "Is Blackstone holding you against your will? You're expendable, you know. Girls like you mean nothing to him. Less than nothing."

Unspeaking, the girl points beneath the bridge, and I gasp. Paige sits on the ground, illuminated by the faint glow from the street above. Still as a stone, her back is braced against a tree trunk. Her head lolls to one side, her face bruised and bloodied.

I start toward the steep embankment.

"Not so fast." The girl withdraws a small handgun, her trembling finger poised on the trigger. "Mr. Blackstone needs the Lolita files. So far, he's been sorely disappointed in your performance."

"Then tell him to man up and come get them instead of sending a little girl to do his dirty work. If he wants the files so badly, he can look me in the eye and tell me himself."

"You're right, Teddy. Can I still call you that?"

I spin around to face Gerald Blackstone, half expecting him to appear the way he did when I saw him last. Standing at the top of my father's staircase, impossibly tanned and broad-shouldered, lording over the party below in his perfectly tailored tux. By that time, I'd already delivered Sidney to the wolves.

"I'd rather you not call me anything."

"You'll always be Teddy to me."

When I look closely, I find his eyes sunken. His body, thinner. Prison whittled him down to sinew and bone. I could break him now. Still, his power wafts from him like a poisonous cologne. It's a fearsome thing to behold.

"Your father told me he nicknamed you Teddy because you reminded him of a little bear toddling after him. You never did live up to his expectations."

"Did you kill him?" When he doesn't answer right away, I plow forward, the words spewing too fast to censor, too fast to control. Each one drips with disgust. "You did, didn't you? You got rid of everybody in your way. My father. Sidney. I saw the video. I know what you've done, you sick bastard. You let Crawley use her and throw her away. Like she was nothing."

"Don't get all high and mighty now, Teddy. You're still the same frat boy you always were, even with your precious PhD. Whatever happened to Sidney, you bear just as much blame as I do. You brought her right to us. As for your father, you can't deny that his death was the best thing that ever happened to you.

You're free now. Well, almost." His lip curling in a sneer, he gazes down below, where Gordo now stands watch over Paige. "Let's not make this any harder than it has to be. You hand over the flash drive and Paige walks out of here. Otherwise . . ."

I lunge toward him, teeth bared.

Blackstone flinches but holds his ground. "I wouldn't do that. You hurt me, he shoots her." He gestures first to Paige, and then to the girl who's positioned herself at my shoulder, aiming her gun at me. "Then she shoots you. It's a bad end all around."

"But it was never going to end well, was it?" I wrap my fingers around the girl's slim wrist, just as I'd done to Lina, to Sidney. Just as I'd seen my father do before me. Pure Drucker, I show no mercy, twisting until she cries out, the gun clattering to the sidewalk.

"Get out of here." I snarl at her, my rage close to the surface. It's a relief to finally let it out, though she doesn't deserve the brunt of it. Collateral damage, she takes off down the street, losing her heels as she runs.

Blackstone watches her for a moment. Mutters under his breath, "Dumb bitch." When he makes a move for the gun, I outfox him, kicking it far out of his reach. I relish his desperation as he scrambles toward it.

"You want the flash drive, don't you?" I shout, stopping him cold. His arm outstretched, he pulls up short, rises slowly. "It's here, your precious snuff film. But you'll never find it without me."

Blackstone shows no alarm, but I can sense it. My father once told me the most fearsome man is the one with nothing to lose.

"What do you want from me?" he asks, raising his hands.

I stalk toward him, retrieving the errant handgun and pointing it at him. "Only what you promised. I'm not giving up anything until Paige is safe with me." Shoving Blackstone to the guardrail, I find Paige again. She's not moving. Her hands, limp in her lap. "How do I know she's alive?"

With a wave from Blackstone, Gordo kicks her foot. A groan escapes her mouth, and she cowers away. It's a gut punch.

"Looks like a live one to me."

"I need to see her for myself." Holding the gun to Blackstone's side, I march him down the steep dirt path that leads to the lawn below. I can hardly look at Paige. Even in the murk, I spot the bruises on her neck. She briefly raises her pained eyes to mine, then drops her gaze back to the ground. At least she's still breathing.

"Alright, sweetheart," Gordo growls at her, dragging her up by the arm and holding on tight.

His fingers leave marks in her flesh, so I dig my nails into Blackstone, keeping him close. It's past time he felt the sting.

"Let's do this nice and easy. No drama," says Gordo.

"Let her go, then I'll give up the drive."

Blackstone nods his agreement, and Gordo nudges Paige forward with the butt of his gun. She hesitates, then wobbles toward me into the dim light. I fight the urge to hold her.

"It's on the east side, the left turret." I gesture back to the bridge, the words tight in my throat. "On top of the ledge. You'll need to stand on the railing to reach it."

Before I finish, Blackstone takes off up the hill, leaving Gordo and his gun behind to keep watch. I stare at Blackstone's back for a moment, imagining myself taking aim. One bullet to the spine, clean through his designer suit, and I'd watch him drop, mortal after all. Whatever happened next, it would be worth it to see him writhe.

Instead, I touch Paige's face. My heart falls when she winces. It's only been two days. It feels like a lifetime. Like she won't know me anymore. Like there's too much to say. Still, I try. "You were right. I'm an idiot."

Paige twists her mouth, shrugs one shoulder. "At least you admit it."

As Blackstone races down the bridge toward the east end, I pull her in, letting her collapse against me. I breathe *I love you* into her hair. It doesn't feel as strange as I thought it would, saying it aloud.

"How touching," Gordo sneers in disgust. "It's *Pretty Woman* come to life. Only you're no Julia Roberts, honey."

My eyes dart over the top of Paige's head to the bridge, where Blackstone has managed to climb atop the concrete railing. He inches forward. Closer, closer. Finally, he places his hand on the tower's ledge, running it along the smooth concrete in search of the flash drive.

When he bellows my name, Paige flinches in my arms. His face, contorted, looming down in the dawn's light like an angry god. "Where is it?"

"Just a little farther to the right."

He shimmies toward the edge of the rail. A sitting duck, ripe for the plucking. Up on his tiptoes now, he scans the ledge.

"Farther . . . farther . . ."

Seizing Paige by the arm, Gordo wrenches her away from me. He grips her in a chokehold and jabs the gun against the side of her head so hard I grimace. When I point mine back at him, he laughs.

"Don't be stupid, Teddy. The deal still stands. If you want her to walk out of here, you play by our rules. Unless you plan to shoot, I suggest you lower your weapon."

"Don't tempt me." But my hand slowly drops.

"You always did think you were so smart. Disappearing like a rat in a hole. Too bad you forgot about facial recognition. Just had to get that driver's license, didn't you?"

Blackstone yowls in frustration from above us, cutting Gordo's rant mercifully short. But his words linger, reminding me I'd been outsmarted, making me doubt myself.

"You liar. Where the hell is it?"

Paige wriggles herself loose and sinks her teeth into Gordo's forearm, drawing blood. Growling, he grapples with her, smacking her across the face.

I watch it all, disbelieving. I'd been wrong about Trevor Dent. I would save her from a burning building. I would rescue her from a pack of wild dogs. I would—

The trigger feels lighter than I expect when I pull it. The wound in Gordo's chest blooms red as a rose. He blinks back at me as he falls, open-mouthed with shock.

Next I take aim at a panicked Blackstone. Fumbling to lower himself from the railing, he nearly loses his balance, making him a moving target.

Before I can pull the trigger again, a sharp blast stuns me. Then another.

I drop to the ground, trying to locate the shooter. Nearby, Paige flattens herself in the grass, looking up at me through the curtain of her hair, her eyes dark pools of terror. A third shot strikes the bridge's tower, splintering the corner of the turret.

"Run," I yell to Paige.

But she shakes her head. "I'm not leaving you."

Trying to regain his balance on the railing, Blackstone teeters and reaches for the ledge. Instead, he grabs a fistful of air and plummets thirty feet to the ground below, landing with a sickening thump beneath the bridge's arch.

In the sudden quiet, I lift my head and scan the ground for the lump of his broken body. He lays, unmoving. Unnaturally still.

Up above, two black-suited men stalk toward the bridge, stopping at the turret. With the grace of a cat, the taller of the two men hoists himself onto the railing and peers atop the ledge. "Not here," he says, returning himself to solid ground.

The men gaze down at us, their faces identical blanks in the dark. Moments later, they begin their descent in unison, revealing more of themselves the closer they come. The matching tridents on their lapels. Glocks, hungry in their hands and aimed at the girl I love.

I turn my eyes away to the steep hillside that leads back to the car. There's a chance to run. To hit the highway and head south. But my feet don't move. I'm rooted here, beneath the Shakespeare Bridge with Paige.

My gun drawn, I face the black suits, two more of Crawley's army. Their eyes glint like steel in the glow of the bridge lights. Their jaws, like chiseled stone. Moving with the swagger of soldiers, I begin to wonder if these men are human at all. If they'd bleed with a bullet to the throat.

"Where are the files?" the taller man snarls at me while the other manhandles Paige to her feet.

"I left the drive on the ledge. Blackstone must have grabbed it before he fell."

Tall Black Suit scowls. Like he's in charge. Like he doesn't believe a word I say.

"No games, I swear. Check him yourself."

While his partner stalks through the grass to Blackstone's body, Tall Black Suit keeps his focus on me and Paige. "Drop your gun. Or she eats a bullet."

Paige nods at me through gritted teeth, and I lay the gun at my feet.

Crouched alongside Blackstone, the second Poseidon goon shakes his head. "It's not here. He's lying."

I shrug, the weight of Paige's life on my shoulders. Sidney's. Lina's too. There's no way I'm letting Crawley's minions anywhere near that flash drive. "Maybe Gordo has it. I mean, he might've—"

"Enough." Tall Black Suit silences me the only way he knows how. With a gun to Paige's forehead. He jabs it so hard against her skin, it leaves a round red mark when he draws it back. He throws her into me, and we both tumble to the ground. "You've got three seconds. Three . . ."

His partner looms in front of me, the barrel of his Glock sizing up my chest.

"Two . . ."

I hear the faint sound of a siren in the distance. Close but not close enough. I reach for Paige's hand.

"One . . ."

Pushing myself up and over, I shield Paige with my body as a hail of gunfire reigns down on us. I lie there with Paige cocooned beneath me, certain I've been hit. Certain it's worth it to know she's still breathing warm against my cheek.

I feel no regret. I feel no pain. Maybe I'm already dead.

"Get up, Trevor."

I roll off Paige toward the sound of a familiar voice and wind up flat on my back staring up at Lina, backdropped by the still-starry sky. When she extends her hand, it feels real in mine. Not dead, then. Not yet.

"In two minutes, this place will be crawling with cops," she says.

"What are you doing here?"

"What does it look like?" she counters, helping Paige to her feet. "I'm saving your ass. Again."

Lina rolls Gordo over, rifling through his pockets. "And taking back what belongs to me."

"You mean what belongs to both of us." I search her eyes for an answer. To the only question that matters to me now. "Did you really intend to sell it to the highest bidder?"

"Of course not." She meets my gaze, then pulls the flash drive from Gordo's pocket and deposits it in hers. "Why would you think that?"

"Because that's what Gordo said. I heard him outside Covington House after you ditched me."

"I told him whatever I had to in order to find you. Poseidon too. They all knew you could locate the files, and so did I. Without you, I would've never found the last piece of the key."

Lina starts up the hillside but turns back when I stay put, my arm around Paige.

"You were right," I tell her, reaching into my sock. "Blackstone made a snuff film."

She stares at the center of my palm, at the second flash drive that's been with me all along. Hidden in plain sight. "I swiped it when you left the room. I needed to know the truth about Sidney."

She nods grimly. "I hope you understand why I ran like I did. I couldn't imagine them getting away with it. With any of it."

"And they won't. You have my word on that."

As the sirens draw nearer, I toss her the keys to the sedan. "Where will you go?" I ask.

She backpedals up the hillside, flashing the secret smile that belongs to her mother. But there's a toughness in her eyes that is hers alone. "Somewhere the past can't find me."

"Take the money in the go-bag. You deserve it. And I don't want it anymore."

Jogging now, she takes one last look over her shoulder. "Want to come?"

I squeeze Paige tight to my side. "I tried that, remember? It's time to stop running. I'm finally ready to be where my feet are."

****

I raise my hands to the sky. Next to me, Paige does the same. On the horizon, the sun finally breaks through, bathing the bridge in soft yellow light. It's the color of hope. Of new beginnings.

"Walk backward toward the sound of my voice."

After a few shaky steps, I find my balance.

"Drop to your knees."

I do as instructed, lowering myself to the cold, hard ground. There will be time to explain, stories to tell. The officer drops a knee on my back, cuffing my wrists.

"What's your name?"

"Teddy Drucker, sir. It's Teddy Drucker."

CHAPTER 27

SEVEN YEARS EARLIER
TEDDY

Teddy chased the melody of Sidney's laughter through the maze. Round and round the hedges they went. Once, she turned and stuck her tongue out at him, waiting until she was just within his grasp to scamper off again. Teddy wondered if she'd had too much champagne. If he'd had too little.

As they neared the fountain, Sidney slowed her pace and turned to him. In the moonlight, her skin glowed, her dress shimmered. Breathless, she stopped by the garden gnome, stooping to rub his hat. "It's lucky, you know."

Teddy reached for her hand, already feeling queasy. "Caught you."

She let him kiss her, soft at first. Then harder. Like his life depended on it. When she pulled away, he spit out the question without thinking. "Did you tip off the police about my father? About Gerry?"

He thought he didn't care about her answer, but when she frowned, hesitated, he felt a fire ignite inside him. Her betrayal burned worse than any other because he hadn't seen it coming. He stalked toward the center of the maze, knowing she'd follow. Knowing Gordo would be waiting there to get to the bottom of this.

"Hold up," she called after him. "Are you mad at me? I thought we agreed. If they're guilty, they deserve whatever they get."

"You want my dad to go to prison?" Teddy asked as the fountain came into view. Gordo stood by the bench, his jaw clenched. Fists balled at his sides.

The moment Sidney laid eyes on him, she balked. "What's this?"

"He just wants to talk to you about what you know. About what you told the police."

"Well, I don't want to talk. Not to him. Ever." Sidney spun away, her dress fluttering behind her like a bright feather. "I'm going back to the house."

Teddy grabbed her by the arm, shocking them both. He told himself to let her go, but his hand kept hold with a mind of its own. "Please. For me. Hear him out. Maybe you didn't see what you thought you did."

Sidney shook her head. He could tell she felt sorry for him. He knew he sounded deluded. The cops had enough evidence to put Gerry away. His father too. But still, couldn't she do this one thing for him?

"Fine. For you, I'll talk to him. But it's not going to change my mind about Gerry. Or your dad. I'm sorry, Teddy. I know you're nothing like them."

The water in the fountain rippled, just as a large koi fish kissed the surface.

"We'll meet Mr. Blackstone in the statuary," said Gordo.

He began to walk, and Sidney trailed behind. Before she disappeared behind the hedge, she glanced over her shoulder, searching Teddy's eyes.

Teddy wanted to reassure her, to go with her. To tell her he'd wait for her inside. But, in the end, he only said, "Goodbye."

CHAPTER 28

FRIDAY MORNING
10 A.M.
LOS ANGELES POLICE DEPARTMENT

I have sandpaper eyes, and a crick in my neck from sleeping in a jail cell. But Paige is safe, and so am I, even if I'm not free to go.

I spent most of the night replaying those final moments beneath the bridge. Gordo, dead. The two Poseidon goons too. Lina, in the wind. I'd watched from the back of a patrol car as the medics strapped Blackstone to a backboard—still breathing—and transported him to the hospital with serious injuries.

When the jailer summons me to the cell front and escorts me back to the interview room, leaving me there hungry and cold, I can guess what it means. Detective Vega has finally arrived from Austin to put me through the gauntlet herself. Never mind that Paige already told them everything. From the kidnapping at the Obsidian—they'd wheeled her out the back entrance in a laundry bin—to the last standoff, where I'd had no choice but to put a bullet in Gordo's heart.

Detective Vega looks as eager as I'd expected. She lives for this kind of thing.

"Well, Doctor Dent, we meet again. Or is it Doctor Drucker?"

"You can call me Teddy." I can't help but smile at her. At her turkey-necked partner too. They've both made the trip to hear me tell the tale. The road I took is littered with dead ends and potholes and head-on collisions. Still, it got me here, and here is not so bad. Here could be worse.

"I got your message," she says. "The laptop you left outside the Santa Monica police station."

I had addressed every word of my confession to Candace Vega, scratching her name and number on the laptop's cover with an ink pen. "And?"

"It's a helluva tall tale. A sex-trafficking real estate mogul. A beautiful paralegal. A snuff film. And a shrink with a new identity. But LAPD tells me your story checks out. That you showed them the evidence to prove it."

Turkey keeps his beady eyes on me, like he still doubts me. Like I might Houdini out of these cuffs at any minute. I nod at him, give him his due.

"What happened to Crawley?" I ask. "Has he been arrested?"

"This morning. The Feds nabbed him at his private hangar. He was about to take a trip to the Maldives. No extradition laws."

Relieved as I am, I wish I could've seen it. The moment it hit him. All his sins come home to roost. "Do you think there's any chance of recovering Sidney's . . . body?"

It still hurts to say it.

Detective Vega sighs. "That will be up to LAPD and the Feds. From what you've shared about Gerald Blackstone, I'd say it's highly unlikely. He doesn't seem like the sort of man who leaves a body behind."

I let it sink in, bone deep.

"I hope it makes sense now. Why I had to come here. After everything I'd done, how I'd hurt Sidney, the role I played in her death, I couldn't let it happen again. Not to someone I love. I did what I had to do to save Paige. Lina and I both did."

Detective Vega remains noncommittal, impossible to read. "And do you know where Lina Carr is now?"

I sigh, remembering the first time she'd rung the bell of Dent Psychotherapy, timid as a mouse. "Just let her be. She's been through enough. Can you blame her for wanting to start over?"

Turkey and Vega exchange a knowing look that sinks my stomach to my knees.

"Did you know she was playing both sides?"

"Meaning?"

"Meaning, we've analyzed telephone records from Lina's hotel room in Austin. She'd been in contact with Erik Gordon. Derek Craig too. We suspect she'd promised your father's files to both, fully intending to double-cross them in the end. Once Gordo caught on, it's no wonder he wanted you to get rid of her."

"Hotel?" It's probably the least of her lies. But I'm back where I started, playing catch-up. Repeating Detective Vega's words like a broken record and scouring Lina's—the seedy motel pool, the sob story about her mom, the panic attacks—for the truth. "I thought she was a student. That's what she wrote on her intake form. *Student.*"

Detective Vega gives me that look. The one saying she feels sorry I'm such a sucker. "Teddy, she's not as innocent as she seems. There's something you should know about the strangling death of your stepmother, Tanya. Vegas PD found a stun-gun mark on her flank. And the only fingerprints on the cord of that hairdryer belonged to Lina."

****

Drucker." The jailer clangs on the bars of my cell, waking me from a half-sleep. "You're free to go."

I change into my old clothes—jeans and the filthy Longhorn sweatshirt Lina picked out at the dollar store—and follow him down the sterile hallway toward freedom, my heart pounding harder than ever.

Because I don't know if Paige will forgive me. If she'll be waiting for me on the other side.

I don't know if we have a shot in hell of making it in the real world. Where life is messy and I'm me and she's her and I'm not a paying customer.

I don't know what will become of Gerald Blackstone. If he'll get what's coming to him, what he deserves. After all, he's an apex predator with a bankroll larger than a small country and a handful of politicians in his pocket.

I don't know if I belong at Dent Psychotherapy. If I belong in Austin. Or Los Angeles. Or somewhere in between. If I can forgive my father, myself.

A single door stands between me and the rest of my life, and I'm scared as hell to open it. The jailer clears his throat, does the job for me. Holding it open, he repeats, "You're free."

I take the first step, inhaling the crisp air of early morning, hopeful that someday, one day, he'll be right.

EPILOGUE

The woman held her head high as she walked, her destination in sight. She looked the part in the pencil skirt and designer heels she'd bought with the money from the go-bag. A white dress shirt, tastefully unbuttoned, revealed her newly tanned skin. Armed with her identification, two large suitcases, and an account number, she smiled at the man who held the door for her, even as his eyes lingered on her breasts. Usually, a man like him made her skin crawl, but nothing could steal her joy. Not today.

Her heels clicked against the marble floors as she approached the desk where she spoke to another man who smiled at her, calling her a most-valued customer. She told him her name was Felicia. She'd chosen it carefully.

Even though she didn't believe in luck, that single night in December when she'd cornered Sidney Archer in the bathroom had revealed itself as her four-leaf clover. Her lucky-seven roll of the dice. She'd been fishing for money, of course. Dangling her tears as bait. Never dreaming she'd hook the mother lode.

Seven. Seven long years she'd waited, biding her time until she could do it right. Give him—all of them—everything they deserved. She knew the money would still be waiting there. Even if the Feds had gotten wind of it, Blackstone had hidden his loot too far for the long arm of U.S. justice to reach. And that greedy pig wouldn't have trusted anyone to move it in his absence.

Felicia informed the private banker of her intentions. A liquidation of the Errinyes account in the sum of ten million dollars. Then she produced the account number she'd carefully transcribed from the spreadsheet and typed in the password she'd committed to memory. She left Gerald Blackstone a single screw-you penny and departed the Bank of Grand Cayman wheeling her cash-lined suitcases.

Afterward, she changed into a dress the vibrant blue of the ocean and found a quiet table at a restaurant overlooking the beach. She opened her laptop and composed a group email, with a link to a file-sharing account that contained the Errinyes financials and every last one of the seedy blackmail videos Blackstone had directed. On the TO line, she added a saved list of contacts. Editors at the *New York* and *LA Times* and the *Wall Street Journal*. Producers at all the major networks. The Director of the FBI. And a special BCC to Trevor Dent Psychotherapy. The poor sap.

Her life's work finally complete, she ordered a bottle of the restaurant's finest champagne. Downing the glass in two swallows, she could barely hide her exhilaration. She could go anywhere. Be anyone she wanted.

"To luck," she said, clinking an imaginary glass against hers.

Felicia left cash on the table and disappeared down the beach, ditching her shoes and leaving her soft footprints in the sand. Come morning, there would be no trace.

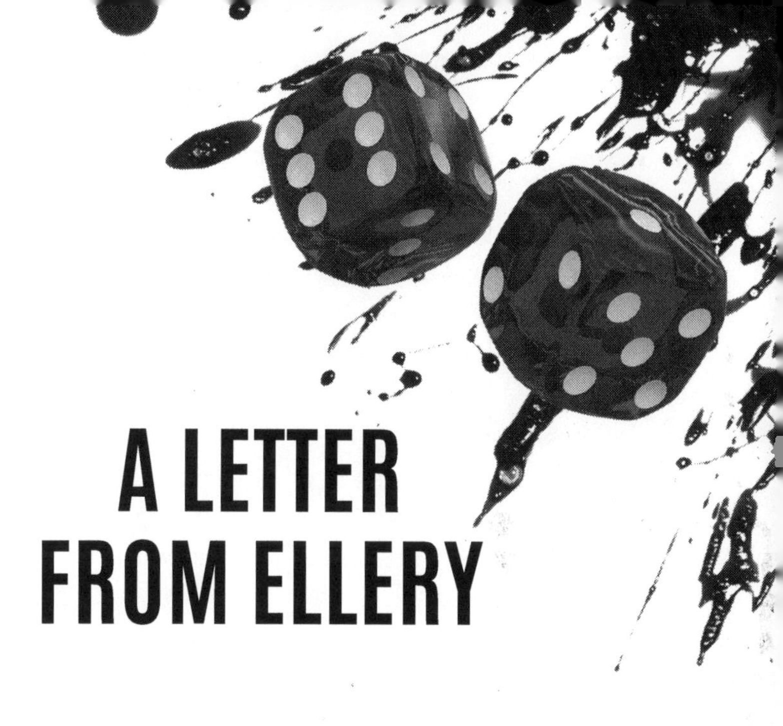

A LETTER FROM ELLERY

Thank you for reading *Lucky Girl*! With so many amazing books to choose from, I truly appreciate you taking the time to read the fifth installment in the Doctors of Darkness series.

In July of 2019, American financier, Jeffrey Epstein, was arrested on federal charges of sex trafficking minors in Florida and New York, in a case that captivated the nation both for its seedy nature and its cinematic ending. But it wasn't Epstein's first brush with the law. In 2008, he'd been convicted on solicitation and prostitution charges involving a fourteen-year-old victim. Though over thirty other victims were identified at the time, he only served thirteen months in custody as part of a controversial plea deal. Epstein was found dead in his jail cell on August 10, 2019, but the mystery surrounding his life and death continue, in part due to his high-profile associates like Donald Trump and Prince Andrew. But perhaps the most enigmatic character to emerge was Ghislaine Maxwell, a woman who allegedly manipulated and trafficked underage girls on Epstein's behalf as part of their complicated decades-long relationship. In writing Lucky Girl, I drew inspiration from Epstein's sordid tale, hoping to give readers a more satisfying ending than his victims who were never able to face him in court or to see him held accountable for his crimes.

One of my favorite parts about being an author is connecting with readers like you. You can get in touch with me through any of the social media outlets below, including my website and Goodreads page. Also, if you wouldn't mind leaving a review or recommending the Doctors of Darkness series to your favorite readers, I would really appreciate it! Reviews and word-of-mouth recommendations are essential, because they help readers like you discover my books.

Thank you again for your support! I look forward to hearing from you, and I hope you'll join me on my next dark adventure.

ACKNOWLEDGMENTS

I started writing *Lucky Girl* almost two years ago. About forty pages in, I myself got lucky, when I signed a publishing contract with Bookouture for my Rockwell and Decker series. For over a year I had no choice but to set aside Trevor and Lina's adventure, and sometimes I wondered if I'd ever have a chance to finish. But like all stories, this one demanded to be told, even if it came about at its own glacier pace, and I hope you enjoyed it.

I owe a tremendous debt to Ann Castro at AnnCastro Studio who provided developmental and line editing services for the book; Lauren Finger who contributed proofreading services; Giovanni Auriemma who always produces the covers of my dreams-nightmares; and Mallory Rock who designed the book's amazing interior. As always, I owe a debt of gratitude to my friends, family, and colleagues—my cheerleaders—who are always there telling me to keep writing and keep dreaming big, as well as my partner in crime and life, Gary. And of course, to you, dear readers, for devouring every sinful bite of the Doctors of Darkness series!

ALSO BY ELLERY KANE

Lucky Girl is the fifth installment in the Doctors of Darkness series of psychological thrillers by forensic psychologist and author, Ellery Kane. If you want to be the first to know when new books are released, sign up for Ellery's newsletter at ElleryKane.com.

If you enjoyed *Lucky Girl*, look for these other great reads from Ellery Kane.

Doctors of Darkness Series

Daddy Darkest

The Hanging Tree

The First Cut

Shadows Among Us

Lucky Girl (A Dose of Darkness Novella)

Rockwell and Decker Series

Watch Her Vanish

Her Perfect Bones

One Child Alive

Legacy Series

Legacy

Prophecy

Revelation

Made in the USA
Las Vegas, NV
15 August 2022